P9-DBX-692

camp CONFIDENTIAL

IN IT TO WIN IT

GROSSET & DUNLAP
Published by the Penguin Group
Penguin Group (USA) Inc., 375 Hudson Street,
New York, New York 10014, USA
Penguin Group (Canada), 90 Eglinton Avenue East, Suite 700, Toronto,
Ontario M4P 2Y3, Canada (a division of Pearson Penguin Canada Inc.)
Penguin Books Ltd., 80 Strand, London WC2R 0RL, England
Penguin Group Ireland, 25 St. Stephen's Green, Dublin 2, Ireland
(a division of Penguin Books Ltd.)
Penguin Group (Australia), 250 Camberwell Road, Camberwell, Victoria
3124, Australia (a division of Pearson Australia Group Pty. Ltd.)
Penguin Books India Pvt. Ltd., 11 Community Centre,
Panchsheel Park, New Delhi—110 017, India
Penguin Group (NZ), 67 Apollo Drive, Rosedale, North Shore 0632,
New Zealand (a division of Pearson New Zealand Ltd.)
Penguin Books (South Africa) (Pty.) Ltd., 24 Sturdee Avenue,
Rosebank, Johannesburg 2196, South Africa

Penguin Books Ltd., Registered Offices:
80 Strand, London WC2R 0RL, England

Cover design by Ching N. Chan
Front cover images © Corbis Photography/Veer Incorporated
and © iStockphoto.com/Nick M. Do.

Library of Congress Cataloging-in-Publication Data is available.

ISBN 978-0-448-45402-3   10 9 8 7 6 5 4 3 2 1

camp CONFIDENTIAL

IN IT TO WIN IT

by Melissa J. Morgan

Grosset & Dunlap
An Imprint of Penguin Group (USA) Inc.

PROLOGUE

Posted by: Avery
Subject: What I'm Wearing Update

Just returned from shopping with my stepmom, Elise, and the peanut, who is getting cuter by the day. Strangers kept stopping us to say how beautiful my little sis is, and to say how much she looks like me. My shopping mojo was strong. I found the perfect sweater for the Walla Walla winter reunion. Cashmere. Black—you know how good I look in black. Rib banded crewneck, cuffs, and hem. With a tree—flat, brass-tone studs—on the back. I can't wait for you all to see me in it.

On the topic of fashion, be prepared to see boys in skirts. It's a tradition at Walla Walla winter reunions that the boys always dress up as cheerleaders for the powder-puff football game (also a tradition) while the girls play against Camp Talamini. Well, some girls. I don't. I will watch, wearing something gorgeous.

I can hardly believe you former Lakeviewers have never been to one of WW's winter reunions, when I've been to so many. It was awful when last year's got canceled because they couldn't work out how to get the camp winterized in a greenie-friendly way.

Secret? I'm glad the winterization problem still isn't quite solved. I'm looking forward to staying at the lodge. Have you seen the pics?

See you all soon, soon, soon!

Kisses,

Avery

Posted by: Sarah
Subject: Football

Powder-puff football? Awesome. Boys in skirts— also nice.

FYI, I am a pass-catching machine. Just sayin'.

Sars

Posted by: Sloan
Subject: SNOW

Is anyone else having trouble getting the parental okay to go to the reunion? My parents are worried about a big snowstorm that's supposed to be heading Connecticut's way over Presidents' Day Weekend, otherwise known as our reunion. They're not sure they want me flying in from Arizona.

I think so much time living in the desert has made them snowaphobes.

Peace, love, and light,

Sloan

Posted by: Chelsea
Subject: What I'm Wearing

I know that sweater, Avery. I know, because I have that sweater. (You described it perfectly, BTW.) I also bought it for the reunion. My question for you— when exactly did you buy it? Because whoever bought it second has to take it back. Or at least not even think about packing it for the weekend.
Chelsea

Posted by: Natalie
Subject: snowaphobe

i feel you, sloan. my dad has lived in lala too long. in la, people have trouble even driving in the rain. seriously. anyway, he didn't want me flying from nyc to connecticut. i think he was having flashbacks to that time his plane went down in the himalayas. i keep telling him—dad, that wasn't your real life. it was a movie. he's picturing me toeless from frostbite, eating my leather boots to stay alive.

fortunately, my mom is a) used to snow, b) not a crazy actor with way too much imagination. we tag-teamed my dad, and he has reluctantly agreed that i can go to the reunion. but he keeps sending me supplies—like a pair of battery-operated heated socks. tell your parents you can wear them, sloan.

love you all. mean it.
nat

Posted by: Joanna
Subject: Don't think I'm crazy

But I feel the same way Nat's dad does. I don't want to freeze and starve and lose even a baby toe. I want to see you all. I do. But I'm thinking maybe I should skip the reunion.

My mom, however, says I should go. Make that, my mom says I am going.

Joanna

Posted by: Avery
Subject: What I'm Wearing

Chels, you wanted to know when I got my fabulous, beautiful sweater. Answer—I bought it an entire day before you bought yours.

Posted by: Jenna
Subject: I will hunt you down

I call quarterback!

And, Joanna, if you don't come, I will hunt you down. Believe it! Same goes for you, Sloan. Do whatever you have to to get your parents to say yes!

Jenna

Posted by: Chelsea
Subject: Receipt

Avery, I'm going to need you to scan your

sweater receipt (which will have a date of purchase on it) and post it.

    Chelsea

    P.S. I didn't actually say when I bought my sweater.

Posted by: Sloan
Subject: Doom

    My parents have decided they don't want me to go to the reunion in case there's a massive snowstorm. I'm going to need ammo to convince them to change their minds. Help! Strategies, suggestions, lies, bribes— I'm open to almost anything. I don't want Jenna to hunt me down. That's scary. And I really, really don't want to miss our reunion. That would be too sad. Too, too sad.

    Sloan

chapter ONE

As soon as Sloan typed a "w" in the Google search box, weatherwatch.com came up in her browser history. Right at the top. She'd been compulsively checking the site for a day and a half, looking for a prediction that would make her parents change their minds and give her the okay to fly off to the Walla Walla reunion over Presidents' Day Weekend.

Please, please, please, she thought as she clicked it, then typed in the zip code for the Connecticut lodge near camp where the reunion was going to be held. Holding her breath, she scanned the ten-day forecast. There was a 65 percent chance of a snowstorm over the long weekend—same as when she'd checked the site yesterday.

Sloan let out the breath. Sixty-five percent. Those odds weren't so bad, and she couldn't wait around to see if they would get better. It was time to go make her plea to her parents.

But first—she moved her mouse over to her "favorites" and clicked the link to the camp blog. She'd posted a message asking for advice on the parent sitch, and wanted to see if any of her friends had come up with anything. She smiled when she saw Avery had posted an answer. Avery was good at getting what she wanted. Sloan eagerly read the message.

Posted by: Avery
Subject: Doom

Sloan, here's my advice: whine and beg. Maybe pout a little. (But not so much that you make your parents so mad they'll never say yes.) If you can do it right, cry some. Play your parents against each other. Basically, just manipulate, manipulate, manipulate.
Avery

Hmmm. Sloan wasn't a drama kind of girl. She was pretty sure that she couldn't squeeze out even one really good fake tear.

Jenna had posted a reply, too. She wasn't the actress type, either. Maybe her advice would be easier to follow. Sloan clicked on her message and read it.

Posted by: Jenna
Subject: Doom

My dad is a stats guy. The stats look okay, he's okay. Use them on your parents, Sloan.

And remember, if you don't get your behind to the lodge, I will hunt you down. And it won't be pretty!

I threaten cuz I love.
Jenna

Statistics, Sloan could handle. She checked a few more websites and memorized a few facts that she thought could help her make her case, then she headed to the kitchen. Her mom was pulling a tofu lasagna out of the oven. Her dad was tossing one of his special salads, this one with cranberries and pecans. Sloan hesitated in the doorway, watching them. *I think it's safe for me fly to Connecticut.* That's what she meant to say. But the words that came out of her mouth were, "I think I'll make us fuzzy orange smoothies to go with dinner," which made her parents happy because they loved Sloan's smoothies. She walked over to the fridge and started pulling out Greek yogurt and the other ingredients she'd need. Why was she so nervous? Her parents were hardly beasts.

Sloan knew the answer. Her parents weren't beastly, but they still might not change their minds. They might give Sloan the "no" again. And Sloan wasn't ready to hear it if they did. She couldn't wait all the way until summer to see her camp friends again. That was months and months away—forever in friend time.

Okay, during dinner, while they're enjoying the smoothies, I'll ask, Sloan promised herself. She was putting orange sections into the blender when the back door flew open. Willow, Sloan's aunt, rushed in. "I got the last loaf of rosemary bread. Score!" She waved her reusable mesh shopping bag over her head in triumph.

"I didn't know you were coming for dinner," Sloan said, grabbing some cinnamon from the cabinet above the blender.

"I invited myself right this second," Willow answered. "But I brought bread. That means I'm welcome."

"You're always welcome. Knowing you, you'd never eat if you didn't want to see us once in a while," Sloan's mom told her. Willow was her younger sister, and sometimes her mom acted like Willow was younger than Sloan.

"You're right. I couldn't live without you. I'd wither away." Willow gave Sloan's mom a hug, shooting a wink at Sloan.

"Very funny. I give out love and concern and I get mocked for it," Sloan's mom said, trying to sound mad, but smiling. "Okay, everyone, let's get the food on the table."

Sloan poured the smoothie into four glasses and carried them to the big table that dominated one side of the huge main room. She loved the big old table, especially the way it matched the massive exposed beams of the ceiling. But as much as she loved the room, and her parents, and her aunt, and tofu lasagna, and fuzzy orange smoothies, she felt nervous. *Not beasts*, she reminded herself, taking her usual seat.

A conversation started up about the new sculpture being installed in Sedona's arts and crafts village. Sloan *uh-huhed* and *mm-hmmed* her way through it, not able to concentrate. She was shocked when she realized she was halfway through her lasagna and had already finished her salad. She didn't remember tasting a bite.

Do it! she ordered herself. *Just do it, or dinner will*

be over and any smoothie magic you had going will be gone. "I have something I wanted to talk to you about," she blurted.

"You just interrupted your aunt," her dad pointed out.

"Sorry, Willow," Sloan said. "What were you saying?"

"Doesn't matter. From the look on your face, you have something important going on," Willow answered.

"I . . . you . . . Weatherwatch . . ." She'd lost contact with the part of her brain that could form sentences. She took a breath, then tried again. "I wanted to let you know that the weather forecast is predicting a sixty-five percent chance of snow in Connecticut over the long weekend. That's not bad, right? Sixty-five percent?"

Willow's eyes began to gleam. "In 2002, there was a freak snowstorm in North Carolina. There was only an eight percent chance it would hit, but it did. Knocked out electricity all over the place. I didn't know you've gotten into meteorology," she added.

"She's gotten into wanting to go to her camp reunion," Sloan's dad said, smiling sympathetically at Sloan.

"Of course. I don't know why I didn't make that connection right away when you said *Connecticut*," Willow answered.

Her aunt was an extreme weather junkie. Sloan hadn't factored that in when she was prepping for this conversation, because she hadn't expected Willow to be there. Maybe she could turn it to her advantage.

"There probably won't be a snowstorm, but if there is, it could be awesome to experience it, right,

Willow? You go all over the place chasing storms so you can see the"—Sloan searched her mind for the phrase her aunt always used—"wildness and majesty of nature."

Sloan's mother groaned. "Please don't use your aunt as an example of sensible behavior," she said.

"Only forty people died last year from a lightning strike!" Sloan exclaimed, trying a new tactic. Her parents and Willow stared at her. Oh, wait. Wrong statistic. *Get it together*, she ordered herself. "I mean, only 449 people died of hypothermia."

"We aren't worried you're going to freeze to death, Sloan," her dad said.

"Well, we are a little," her mother corrected.

"But we're more worried about things like your connecting plane being delayed by the weather," Sloan's dad continued. "We don't want you sitting all by yourself in an airport in a city where you know no one."

"Or getting snowed in at that lodge, which is in the middle of nowhere," her mother added.

So much for stats, Sloan thought. She decided to try a little of Avery's advice. "Please let me go. Just please." *I'm not all that good at begging*, she realized.

To her surprise, he father turned to her mother. "I checked a couple weather sites, too," he told her. "Like Sloan said, there's only a little more than a fifty-fifty chance there will be a snowstorm. And if there is, it's not a given that any of the airports will have to delay flights more than a few hours."

"We've already decided this. She's not going,"

Sloan's mom protested.

"Maybe we should rethink it," her dad said.

Yes, yes, yes! Sloan thought. "What do you think, Willow?" she asked eagerly. She didn't want to play her parents against each other. But getting her aunt to agree with her dad couldn't hurt.

Willow didn't answer. She was fiddling with her BlackBerry. "What do you think, Willy?" Sloan asked again.

Willow frowned, eyes still on her BlackBerry screen. "Connecticut had unusually hot weather summer before last," she said.

"See! Unusually warm weather! That means no snow!" Sloan cried.

"Actually, it means the opposite. Many times where there's an unusually hot summer someplace there is an unusually bad winter there sixteen months later," Willow said. She shook her head. "I'm not happy with what I'm seeing on bird migration patterns. Hibernation data, either. And the wind patterns— cold wind is going to be shooting into Connecticut over the weekend. I don't think that there's a sixty-five percent chance of a snowstorm. I think there's more like a ninety-eight percent chance." She looked over at Sloan. "Sorry, sweetie. But the birds and bears know the score."

"Willow agrees with me," Sloan's mom said. "It's settled."

"No. Wait!" Tears actually did begin to sting Sloan's eyes as she thought about missing the chance to be with her friends. There had to be a way to turn this around. She began to talk. And talk. And talk.

An hour later, Sloan flopped into the chair in front of her computer. She felt drained. Her throat felt raw from all the talking. She logged onto the camp blog and began to type.

Posted by: Sloan
Topic: Parents

I'm too tired to write much. But I had to tell you all that—wait for it—I'm coming to the reunion! Woo-hoo! Nat—I hope you were serious about your offer to share your electric socks with me. I think my access to those socks helped tip my mom into the "yes" zone.

Peace, love, and light (and no snowstorms),
Sloan

▲ ▲ ▲

"Peter, what do you have lined up for the long weekend?" his dad asked as he helped himself to a second slice of olive and pepperoni pizza.

"Movie mar-a-thon! I'm going to watch every Jimmy Stewart western," Peter answered. "I've never seen any of them, and I read this Clint Eastwood quote that said no one was as good a bad guy as Stewart. I want to see it for myself."

Peter's twin sister, Avery, gave one of her disdainful half sniff/half snorts. His father and Elise, his stepmom, exchanged a not-happy-with-that-answer look. No one in his family understood that, for Peter, watching movies wasn't just *watching movies*. He wanted to be a great actor, and one of the ways he was going to make that happen was by viewing the performances of the great actors of the past. Was that so hard to understand?

"Not going to meet up with Zack or one of your other friends?" his dad asked.

Peter took a crust of pizza off Avery's plate and popped it into his mouth. She narrowed her eyes at him, even though he knew for sure she wasn't going to eat the crust herself. She hated crusts. She said even the word "crust" was disgusting.

He took his time chewing, trying to figure out what to say to his father. Finally, he shrugged. "Maybe. I haven't talked to them about it. We're guys. If we want to do something, we text each other three minutes before."

"Zack won't be around," Avery said. "Becca told me that her whole family is going skiing in Tahoe."

"Your dad told me you were pretty into skiing a few years ago," Elise commented. "Is that something you'd like to do? I bet I could still book us something. The baby and I can sit by the fire, and you and your dad could hit the slopes."

"I'm good," Peter told her. "I'm really into the Stewart thing." His parents exchanged another look.

"I was on the phone with Dr. Steve—"

"Dr. Steve?" Avery exclaimed. "Why?"

"Who's Dr. Steve?" Peter asked.

"He runs Camp Walla Walla," Elise answered.

Peter's parents had signed him up to go to the camp in the summer—without bothering to consult him. Apparently, they didn't think he was social enough or something. Peter disagreed, but there wasn't much he could do about it.

"All the stuff Avery's been telling us about the winter reunion sounded really good," Peter's dad continued. "I wanted to see if new campers could go."

Peter did not like the sound of that.

Neither did Avery.

"It's a reunion," she pointed out. "By definition a reunion is for old campers."

"Dr. Steve said that any new campers who are signed up to go to Walla Walla in the summer are also welcome," his dad said.

"It would be a great way for you to get to know some people you'll be hanging out with over the summer," Elise added. "Avery can introduce you to everybody."

Avery didn't comment.

"Since you don't have plans, I'm going to sign you up," his dad announced.

"I do have plans, though," Peter protested. "I told you." His voice came out sounding kind of whiny. That wasn't going to help him make his case. He tried again. "You know how much I want to be an actor," he said, trying to keep his voice calm and even. "It takes a ton of work. I need to keep putting in the hours."

"Yeah, Peter's been all about acting for a long time now. You should be proud he's been putting so much effort into it," Avery said. Peter knew that she was only saying that because she didn't want him crashing her reunion. He didn't care. He'd take backup wherever he could get it.

"One weekend off isn't going to hurt you," his father said. "It will be good for you to get out with other kids."

"We do think it's great how devoted you are to acting," Elise chimed in. "But it's good to have some balance. If you had plans . . ." She let her words trail off.

Peter wondered if it would be worth making up some plans. But Zack wasn't the only one going away for the weekend. Most of his other friends were, too. And going skiing with his dad and Elise just didn't sound that fun.

"Fine. I'll go," he said. Because he knew he had to do something this weekend. Something other than what he actually wanted to do.

"Great!" Elise exclaimed. "Avery will make sure you meet everyone, right, Ave?"

"Absolutely," Avery answered, sounding deeply and absolutely unenthused. So what? If he was going to have to spend the weekend doing stuff he didn't want to, why should she get to be happy?

▲ ▲ ▲

When her parents were all caught up watching a DVD about teaching babies—yes, babies—to read, Avery headed to her brother's room. She knocked on Peter's door, then walked in without waiting for him to answer.

"Do come in," Peter snarked.

Avery sat down in his desk chair. "Look, I'll introduce you to some of the guys, but you're mostly going to be on your own, you know that, right?"

"Whatever," Peter said. "I'm going to bring my portable DVD player and some movies. Not the westerns, though. I need to really be able to concentrate on them the first time I watch them."

"Against the rules. We don't get to use cell phones, so forget about DVD players or computers," Avery told him. Peter looked so disappointed she felt a little bad for him. She didn't want her brother at the reunion, but maybe it would be good for him. If he kept acting like an antisocial loser, he might end up a complete freak who would never be able to talk to anyone.

She used her feet to twirl Peter's desk chair from side to side. "You better hope Sarah, Natalie, and Brynn don't tell everyone what happened last fall."

Peter, Sarah, and Brynn had been extras in a movie together. Peter had lied to them—big-time lied—as part of this ridiculous plan he'd come up with to break into the movie biz. He'd even lied about his name. Or at least he hadn't told them that Chace was his stage name, not his real name.

"I'm incredibly popular at Walla Walla," Avery continued. "But you're going to need more than an incredibly popular sister if that story gets around."

"Natalie and Sarah are going to be there?" Peter leaped up from his bed, as though saying their names had given him an electric shock.

"Uh . . . yeah. What part of Walla Walla winter reunion didn't you understand?" Avery answered.

"I just—I don't know. I wasn't thinking about it. I didn't even know I was going to the reunion until about a half hour ago." Peter began pacing back and forth in front of her.

"Don't have a panic attack," Avery told him, feeling a spurt of pity for her twin. "Just find Nat and Sarah as soon as we get to the lodge and apologize. They'll be cool about it." Avery knew firsthand that Natalie and Sarah could be forgiving. She hadn't exactly been nice to either of them when they first started at Walla Walla, but they'd all ended up friends.

Peter kept pacing. "Impossible. I made Sarah think I liked her just so her dad would cast me in a movie. Well, the guy I *thought* was her dad. Girls don't forget stuff like that," he said.

"You really did hurt her," Avery said. "I don't know why, but she actually liked you back."

"And Natalie. She acted like I'd treated her exactly the same way." Peter slumped back down on the bed.

"You sort of did," Avery told him. "You sucked up to Sarah because you thought she was Tad Maxwell's daughter. Then you dumped her when you found someone you thought could help your *so-called* movie career. That's something that's happened to Natalie, too. Because her dad *is* Tad Maxwell."

"But I didn't do that to her," Peter protested.

"Are you saying you wouldn't have acted that way if you'd known she was really Tad Maxwell's daughter?" Avery asked. She waited for Peter to answer, and shook her head when he didn't. "You would have tried to play her the way you played Sarah."

"I guess," Peter admitted, looking down at the carpet, as if he were talking to it instead of Avery.

"So apologize," Avery said. "Nobody likes to do it, but sometimes you just have to suck it up."

"I can't. They wouldn't let me. They both hate me too much," Peter answered. "I'll just avoid them. Brynn, too. I didn't exactly do anything to her, but she was there. She was a witness."

"Bad idea," Avery answered. She knew Sarah and Natalie and Brynn. She knew everyone at camp. Which meant she knew exactly how bad an idea it was. But if her brother didn't want to listen to her wisdom, he'd have to deal with the consequences.

chapter TWO

Joanna opened the medicine cabinet in her mother's bathroom. She found the thermometer and stuck a bright pink Post-it note on it that said: Call the doctor if temperature over 101°F.

She walked into her mom's bedroom and found her mother's five pound weights. She stuck a Post-it on each of them. Both notes said: No heavy lifting.

Where should I put the note about chills? she asked herself. Hot water bottle? The warm hand-knit blanket her mother always pulled out when Joanna was sick? Her mom's flannel bathrobe? Joanna decided on all three. She began to write out the notes: Call doctor if you get a chill.

"Joanna! Come on. Your dad's here to drive you to the reunion!" her mother called up the stairs.

Joanna finished scribbling the three notes as fast as she could, then raced around, putting the Post-its in the spots she'd picked. Next, she dashed to her room and grabbed her suitcase and her parka. Her gloves and scarf were in her parka pockets. She was heading down the front stairs when her mother called her again.

"Right here!" Joanna answered, rolling her suitcase toward the door.

"Have a wonderful time, sweetie." Her mom gave her a hug.

Joanna thought of a Post-it that should go on the fridge. "Mom, remember to call the doctor if you stop being able to eat or drink liquids."

"Got it," her mother answered.

"And don't forget to check the incision," Joanna added. "If it gets red or gets bigger, call the doctor. Or if there's purulent drainage."

"Otherwise known as gross, but ordinary, pus," her mom said. "Jo-Jo, I had my gallbladder removed. People get their gallbladders removed all the time. I'll be fine."

"I know. But I'd rather just stay home this weekend. Just in case," Joanna answered. Even with all the Post-its, she felt nervous. "What if—"

She was interrupted by two quick honks. "Your dad's waiting. Go on." Her mother nudged her toward the door. "Believe it or not, I managed to keep myself alive for quite a few years before you came along. Not that I don't appreciate all your mother-henning."

Joanna hesitated. It felt like her feet had grown into the floor. How was she supposed to move? Her mother gave her a little nudge, and suddenly her feet were free. "Okay, well, bye, Mom. See you in a few days." A few days when all kinds of bad things could happen. Joanna had memorized the entire list her mom's doctor had given her mother.

"Bye! Have a great time!" her mother called as Joanna rolled the suitcase out the door. A few seconds later, Joanna heard the door shut behind her.

"What were you doing in there? Making all your own clothes for the weekend?" her father teased, coming halfway up the front walk to meet her. He grabbed her suitcase, tossed it in the trunk, and then he and Joanna got in the car. "Excited about the reunion?" he asked as they pulled out of the driveway.

"Sure," Joanna answered. She'd meant to sound cheery, but the word came out flat and sad.

"Sure," her dad repeated, doing an exaggerated impression of her.

Joanna smiled a little. "I'm just worried about Mom being home alone. There are all these things that could happen where she's supposed to call the doctor. What if she forgets one?"

"Your mom doesn't forget much," her father answered. He had that tone—that divorced person tone. Joanna had heard it a lot over the last seven months.

"Dad, why didn't you come to the hospital when Mom was having her surgery?" Whoops. Joanna hadn't exactly been planning to ask him that, even though she'd been thinking about it a lot. Once it was out there, though, she figured she might as well say everything she wanted to. "I mean, you and Mom keep telling me that you're friends. But if that's true, you would have been there."

Her father sighed. He fiddled with the volume on the radio, then sighed again.

Joanna felt a little spurt of guilt. She'd known this would be a not-happy conversation. That's why she'd pretty much decided not to have it. Until the blurt.

"I think it's more that we both want to be at the point where we're friends," her dad finally said. "But we're not quite there. We will be, though. It'll just take us some time."

Joanna nodded, but it didn't exactly make sense. If two people both wanted to be friends, why couldn't they just . . . be friends?

"And just so you know," her father added. "I wanted to be at the hospital. I wanted to be there with you. But your mother didn't want me there, and your uncle was there, and Barbara, too, right?"

"Right," Joanna added. She was sure they'd both check on her mom while she was away, too. It wasn't the same as living with her, though. If Joanna had stayed home, she'd have been able to be with her mom every minute.

"So, license plate game?" her dad asked.

Joanna wasn't so sure. The license plate game was a family thing, a tradition since Joanna was a little kid. This was the first car trip she and her dad had taken solo since the divorce. They'd driven around town together, but that was it.

"Florida!" he father called out.

If nothing else, maybe the game would keep Joanna's mind away from that list of symptoms that meant her mother needed to call the doctor. She started checking the license plates of the cars going by. More quickly than she expected, the lodge came into view. It looked kind of like a huge, huge barn. It was painted a deep red, with white trim around the windows.

"Twenty-six to twenty. I still rule," her father announced when they pulled up in front of the lodge. "This place looks awesome."

Joanna looked at the big WELCOME WALLA WALLA CAMPERS! banner over the main door. *All your friends are going to be here*, she reminded herself. *There are going to be boys wearing cheerleader skirts. There's going to be nonstop fun.*

But somehow, she didn't feel like getting out of the car. She felt like asking her dad to turn around and drive her back home to her mom.

▲ ▲ ▲

"I'm here! I'm here! I'm really and truly here!" Arms flung out, Sloan spun around in a circle in the main room of the lodge. She loved the wide plank floors. She loved the cozy plaid couches. She loved the massive fireplace that was almost big enough to stand in. Well, if there wasn't a beautiful fire already going. She loved that, too!

"You're here!" Natalie cried as she and Jenna raced down the wide staircase toward Sloan.

"You didn't make me hunt you down. Smart girl," Jenna said as Sloan tried to hug her and Natalie at the same time.

"Come on and see the upstairs," Natalie urged. "We're four in a room. Well, five in some rooms, but four in the one we're in. And guess what? Ellie's here!"

"Cool," Sloan said as she started up the stairs, her duffel bag bumping along behind her. Ellie was one of her favorite counselors.

"Boys are in the rooms to left, girls in the ones to

the right," Jenna explained. "Nat and I have already staked out the room closest to the middle."

"We need to be at the center of everything," Natalie added. She opened the door of the room right at the top of the stairs. "One bed left in the prime location. Want it?"

"Absolutely!" Sloan stepped inside and saw Joanna sitting on the bed nearest the window, staring out at the gray day. She had her arms wrapped around herself, and didn't look up as they entered.

"This is a reunion, Joanna!" Sloan called out. "That means you're required to jump up and down and squeal every time a new person arrives."

Joanna jerked to her feet. "I didn't even hear you come in. I was—" She gave a helpless shrug. "I was thinking."

"Well, start squealing," Sloan told her.

"And jumping," Natalie added.

Joanna gave a small, soft squeal, paired with a little hop.

"That was pretty weak," Jenna said.

"Let me show you how it's done." Brynn strode into the center of the room, bounced up and down while spinning in a circle, and let out a long, long, long, loud, loud, loud squeal. Sloan thought it could probably be heard on Broadway, which was where Brynn hoped she'd be performing someday.

"I'm not sure my hearing will return before we go home," Jenna joked, thumping on one ear with the heel of her hand. "But it's great to see you! Woo-hoo! The party's getting started."

"Looks like this room is full," Brynn commented.

"I'm going to go stake out a bed in the one next door. Don't do anything fun until I get back."

"Unpacking doesn't count as fun, does it?" Sloan flung her duffel on the unclaimed bed. She unzipped it and started pulling out clothes.

"There's an empty drawer in the dresser," Natalie said.

"A drawer?" Sloan asked. The tall dresser had six.

"I was here first, I claimed one of the extras," Natalie answered.

Jenna grinned. "She needs it. You know Nat and her wardrobe changes." Jenna pointed to the second drawer from the top. "That one's mine. There's a little extra space in it if you need it. I'm low maintenance, unlike some people."

"One drawer is fine for me. It's Friday. We're leaving Monday night. I didn't bring all that much." She pulled a pair of jeans out of her bag, and found a manila envelope underneath. Huh. She hadn't packed that.

Sloan ripped open the envelope.

"Did you map out some plays for the powder-puff game, too?" Jenna asked. "I couldn't help myself, even though I don't know how Walla Walla does powder-puff, like if the coaches come up with all the plays. Or if there even are coaches."

"It's not plays. It's stuff from my aunt," Sloan said. "Listen to this note. 'Sloan, sweetpea. I hope I'm wrong about the storm. But I don't think I am. (Remember I have consulted the wind, the birds, and the bears.) Here's some info you might need. Hope you don't, but afraid you will.'" Sloan flipped through the stack of info that her aunt had printed out from the Internet.

"She really thinks we're going to get snowed in?" Joanna asked. She pulled her sweater sleeves down over her hands, as if she were already freezing.

Sloan nodded. "And she's some kind of weather expert. Or at least she thinks she is. She loves any kind of storm and is always reading about them. But weatherwatch.com says there's only a sixty-five percent chance we'll get snow. I double-checked before I left. It's part of the reason my parents gave in and let me come."

"What's the other part?" Natalie asked.

"Your electric socks," Sloan answered.

"Got 'em. And extra batteries," Natalie said. "The socks really made them change their mind?"

"That and I convinced them to call Dr. Steve," Sloan said. "He promised I wouldn't be abandoned in a snowdrift if my flight back home was canceled because of a storm. He also promised he'd stocked up on emergency supplies, just in case we got snowed in here."

"I think it would be fun to be snowed in," Jenna said. "We'd get an extra long holiday weekend with our favorite people."

"I don't think it would be all that fun," Joanna answered. "It's cold enough in here already."

"There's a huge fire downstairs," Sloan told her.

"But our beds are up here," Joanna answered.

"What did I miss?" Brynn asked, rushing back into the room.

"Sloan's aunt is a weather geek, and she thinks we might get snowed in this weekend," Natalie said.

"I'd love that." Brynn plopped down on Natalie's bed.

Sloan noticed Joanna's forehead creasing with worry. "It probably won't happen, Joanna. And if it does, I have complete instructions on what to do." She waved the stack of papers her aunt had sneaked into her suitcase.

"Let me see!" Brynn held out her hand, and Sloan passed her the papers.

"Eww," Brynn said a moment later.

"What?" Joanna asked, her voice tense.

"There's an article about frostbite. Did you guys know that your skin cells die if that happens? Ice crystals form on the outside of the cells, which dehydrates the cells and eventually—*kaplooey*," Brynn said. "Not that they actually blow up. But they do die. And the skin gets all black and gross."

"Your aunt is really into storms?" Joanna asked, eyes locked on Sloan.

"Yeah, she even goes chasing after tornadoes," Sloan answered.

"What did she mean about birds and bears?" Joanna pressed.

"She checks all these factors to predict if a storm is coming," Sloan said. "Including when the birds migrate and when the bears go into hibernation."

"And she thinks there's more than a sixty-five percent chance of a snowstorm?"

Joanna sounded really nervous.

"She thinks there's more of a chance than that," Sloan admitted.

"How much?" Joanna asked.

"She's not a meteorologist or anything," Sloan said.

"How much, Sloan?" Joanna's voice rose a little.

"Um, about ninety-eight," Sloan admitted.

"Bring it on!" Brynn exclaimed. "A snowstorm versus the Walla Walla campers? No contest!"

▲ ▲ ▲

"Connor, Miles, David, Justin, Ben," Avery rattled off, pointing to each guy as she said his name. Then she pointed to Peter. "My brother, Peter. He's going to be at Walla Walla this summer, so he came to the reunion."

"Hey," Peter said. The guys *hied*, *hey*ed, and *what's up*ed back.

"Okay, well, I'm going to go unpack." Avery turned and breezed out of the room. She hadn't been kidding about Peter being pretty much on his own.

"You can have that bed," David told him. "Just kick Miles off. He and Connor are hanging in here because they're trying to absorb some of my coolness."

"Actually, we're trying to help *David* not be such a loser," Miles joked. "We're hoping he'll learn by watching us."

"Yeah, we don't want to hurt his feelings by calling him a loser to his face," Connor agreed. He stood up. "He's probably absorbed as much as he can right now." He laughed and turned to Miles. "We have to remember his brain is small. Let's go unpack."

Peter dropped his gym bag and backpack on the bed Miles had vacated. He started pulling out his clothes and DVDs and sticking them in the chest at the foot of his bed, just wanting to have something to do. It was a little awkward hanging out with the guys for the first time, when they all knew one another so well.

Ben suddenly noticed the DVD in Peter's hand. "You brought *Evil Dead 2*? I've watched that with my dad about ninety-seven times," he said. "I even have the T-shirt."

"If it's a beat-up old T-shirt with something on it no one's ever heard of, Ben has it," David commented.

"Take it back," Ben mock-threatened. "Everyone's heard of Frankenberry." He opened his plaid flannel shirt wide to display the faded Frankenberry tee underneath.

"You seriously haven't heard of *Evil Dead 2*?" Peter asked David. "It's a classic." He'd decided to bring some of his all-time favorites. He always liked to watch them when he wasn't feeling well. Not that he was expecting to feel bad this weekend. All he had to do was stick with his avoidance plan and he'd be fine.

"Nope, never heard of it," David answered.

"Me neither," Justin said. "Although my parents are very organic-pomegranate-juice, one-hour-of-PBS-a-day types. Not that I don't hoover up all possible junk food and bad TV when I'm out of their sight. Still, I'm deprived, seriously deprived."

"Oh, man. You guys need to see it," Ben told them. "There's this scene where this guy keeps breaking dishes over his head, because his hand is possessed and it wants to kill him."

Peter loved that scene. The actor, Bruce Campbell, played it perfectly. Peter had watched it again and again, trying to get the guy's moves down. Peter stood up and began staggering around the room, using one hand to hold the other away from him.

He let the hand "escape," grabbed a notebook off Justin's bed, and hit himself over the head with it. Then he snatched a handful of his hair and pretended the hand was forcing his head to slam into the wall again and again and again.

"Who's laughing now?" Ben shouted. He could hardly get the line from the movie out because he was laughing too hard. Justin and David were laughing, too.

Peter sat back down on his bed. "So I guess this means you won't be mentioning the fact that I smuggled in this—" He pulled his portable DVD player out of his backpack.

"Anyone who knows me knows I'm all about the rules," David joked.

Justin bounced a pillow off his friend's head. "What other movies you got in there?" he asked Peter.

This weekend might not be so bad, Peter decided. Well, as long as he could stay away from Natalie and Sarah. He wasn't as worried about Brynn. She was like a second-degree victim. He had treated her friends badly while she'd been around, which was not good—at all—but it wasn't the same as being treated badly herself.

Natalie and Sarah—they were the two who *had* to hate him with extreme hatred. Peter would just stay as far away from them as possible. That was the plan, at least.

chapter

THREE

Avery studied herself in the long bathroom mirror and nodded with satisfaction. Her turtleneck with the asymmetrical hem was perfect to wear to dinner. She gathered her hair into a sleek ponytail and touched up her lip gloss.

"Ten minutes to chow!" Ellie called from the hallway.

I guess I should give Natalie and Sarah a heads up that my evil twin is on the premises, Avery thought. Some surprises could be fun. Seeing Peter wasn't one of them—at least it wouldn't be for Nat and Sarah.

She left the bathroom, wondering how her brother was doing over on the guys' half of the floor. Peter had gotten so into acting and movies, it felt like he'd forgotten how to talk about anything else. She hoped he wasn't summarizing every seventies western or something equally yawn-inducing.

Avery spotted Natalie heading toward the stairs. A few seconds more, and she'd have missed her friend. "Nat!" she called.

Natalie turned around and smiled at Avery. "Nice sweater. Theory, right?"

"Are you ever wrong about clothes?" Avery asked as she walked over. Natalie was one of two camp girls whose appreciation of fashion went as deeply as Avery's own. Chelsea was the other one.

"I once bought a very ugly hat. But I had a fever that day," Natalie joked. "You heading down to the dining room?"

"In a minute. I actually want to talk to you and Sarah for a sec first," Avery answered.

"Oooh. Got gossip?" Natalie asked.

"You could call it that. I guess," Avery answered. Why hadn't her brother just grown a spine and apologized as soon as they got there the way she'd told him he should? "Let's see if Sarah's still in the room."

Avery led the way to the room she was sharing with Sarah, Brynn, Chelsea, and Priya. She opened the door just as Priya was opening it from the other side, with Brynn, Chelsea, and Sarah behind her.

"You guys are going the wrong direction," Brynn said. "The food is that-a way." She pointed out the door.

"We'll meet you down there," Avery answered. "Nat and I just need to grab Sarah for one minute."

Brynn glanced from Avery to Natalie to Sarah. "What's up? Some big secret?"

Natalie shrugged. "I don't know myself."

"Don't look at me," Sarah said.

"Can we hear it? Can we, can we?" Brynn asked. "I don't think I'll be able to eat if I don't know the secret."

"Yes, you will. We're having spaghetti. You love spaghetti," Priya said. "Come on."

"But a secret is even yummier than spaghetti,"

Brynn answered. "Sorry, I know I'm being obnoxious. Just—tell me, tell me, tell me, please, please, please."

Avery laughed. "All right. Let us in and I'll tell you all. It's not much of a secret. Not a secret at all, really. You would probably already know it if you'd just gone straight downstairs."

Brynn, Priya, Chelsea, and Sarah moved out of the doorway, giving Natalie and Avery room to go inside. "I just wanted to let you know that my brother's here," Avery announced. "He's coming to camp this summer, and my parents wanted him to meet some people first."

Sarah sank down on her bed. "Chace? I mean, Peter?" she asked.

"Oh, wow," Brynn said. She looked at Sarah. "Are you going to be okay?"

"You already knew the whole story," Avery said. She turned to Priya and Chelsea. "Brynn and Sarah and my brother were all extras in a movie together the fall before last. And he . . . wasn't the nicest person."

"He made Sarah think he liked her because he thought she was Tad Maxwell's daughter," Brynn added. "So not cool."

Avery felt a little bad. If she'd kept to her plan and pulled Sarah and Natalie aside, maybe the other girls wouldn't have ever heard the story of what he did.

But, this was camp, she reasoned. All the girls were super tight. She decided that, really, there was no way the details about Peter/Chace would have stayed secret.

"It was partly my fault. At least the part about

him thinking I was Tad Maxwell's daughter was," Sarah admitted, her face flushing. "Remember how my first summer at Walla Walla I kind of borrowed Natalie's life . . ."

"And I mentioned Sarah and her superstar dad in a postcard to my brother, because he's so into movies," Avery said. "When I found out Natalie was actually the celebrity spawn, I didn't bother telling him. Or forgot to, is probably more like it."

"So Peter thought getting close to me could help him get a movie career going," Sarah explained. "He really . . . I really thought he liked me."

"Ouch," Priya said, with a grimace of sympathy.

"Very ouchy," Chelsea agreed.

"And he thought he was pretending to like *me*. Well, you know, me the girl who is actually Tad Maxwell's daughter. Which has so happened to me before," Natalie jumped in. "Some actors will do anything to get cast in a movie. Even pretend they're interested in a star's kid."

"And Peter's completely obsessed with being an actor. It's like he thinks his life will be over if it doesn't happen," Avery said. "Not that there's any excuse for doing what he did."

"No excuse," Natalie agreed, her eyes flashing. "Kids of celebs have actual feelings and everything. We aren't just props or accessories. When I get used, it hurts. Sarah knows."

"Thinking that Chace—this supercute, really fun guy—liked me, and then finding out he'd only been faking . . . Natalie's right. It hurt. As in a lot," Sarah said.

Ellie popped her head in the door. "Dinner in three," she told them with a smile.

"On our way," Brynn answered.

"So, that's it. That's all I wanted to tell you," Avery said. "I didn't want you to go into a state of shock when you saw him downstairs."

"I wouldn't have gone into a state of shock," Natalie answered. "I'd have gone into a state of extreme fury. I still might."

"Don't worry," Brynn joked to Avery. "We'll get all the girls to make a human shield between Nat and Sars and your brother if we have to."

For once, Peter might be right, Avery thought. *Maybe staying as far away from Sarah and Natalie as possible is the best plan for him.*

▲ ▲ ▲

"Welcome, Walla Walla-ers!" Dr. Steve cried from the front of the dining room.

"Whoot!" Natalie and the rest of the campers shouted in return. Needless to say, they were all really excited to be back at camp. Well, back with all the camp people. The lodge was about fifteen miles away from the actual camp.

"It's great to see all your faces again," Dr. Steve continued. "You'll notice a few new faces in the group, too. A few campers who'll be joining us at Walla Walla this summer are here for the reunion. Make them feel at home!"

"Do you think Peter would feel at home if I went over there and dumped a plate of spaghetti over his head?" Natalie whispered to Sarah.

Sarah gave a snort of laugher. "Um, no," she whispered back. "But I would very much enjoy seeing it."

"Some of you may have noticed it's a little chilly in here," Dr. Steve went on.

Joanna's hand shot up.

"Question, Joanna?" Dr. Steve asked.

Joanna shook her head. "I was just raising my hand so you'd know that I noticed. I really noticed!"

"The heater in the lodge is being a little uncooperative, but we're on it," Dr. Steve answered. "Now enjoy your dinner. We have some great games and activities planned for later tonight."

Joanna raised her hand again.

"I know—it's still cold," Dr. Steve joked.

"It is," Joanna answered. "But that's not what I was going to say. I wanted to know if you've heard anything about the snowstorm. Do you think we're going to get hit?"

Dr. Steve rubbed the back of his neck. "The reports right now are saying we should get some snow. But not enough to ruin the Walla Walla annual powderpuff football game."

"Yeah!" Priya and Jenna cried out together. They reached across the table and slapped hands.

"I'm excited about it, too, especially since it's the first one for me and the other former Lakeview campers. I'll keep you all updated on the weather," Dr. Steve continued. "And the staff and I have plans in place if we do get snowed in."

Joanna raised her hand again.

"Yes, Joanna?"

"Are part of the plans us going home early?" she asked.

Dr. Steve couldn't answer for a few moments. The *no ways* and *nos* and general wails of protest would have drowned him out.

"I don't see that happening, although there's a slim possibility," Dr. Steve reassured the group. "We have plenty of food and plenty of firewood. Plenty of extra blankets, too. And if we end up snowbound—which isn't likely—we have some great indoor events. It's going to be a great weekend. Go, Walla Walla!"

"Go, Walla Walla!" Natalie chorused along with the rest of her table. Except Joanna. Natalie noticed she hadn't joined in. "You okay, Joanna?" she asked.

"Yeah. I was just thinking maybe Sloan should give Dr. Steve all that info her aunt dug up," Joanna said. "There was a whole article about knowing when to evacuate."

"I'm sure Dr. Steve knows all of it," Sloan answered.

"You're not worried by the fact that your aunt thinks there's almost a hundred percent chance of a snowstorm?" Joanna asked.

"I'm here, that's all I care about!" Sloan answered. "And if I don't get home until April or May, that's okay by me."

"I'll be frozen solid by that time," Joanna mumbled.

A bunch of guys at the next table laughed, but they couldn't have heard what Joanna said. Natalie glanced over in time to see Peter feeding a bite of spaghetti to his ear while giving a silent, open-mouthed scream.

What an idiot, she thought. Miles, David, Ben, and Justin didn't seem to think so, though. They were laughing like they'd never seen anything so funny. Even Jackson—who, as a counselor, was supposed to set a good example and all—was laughing.

Avery covered her face with her hands. "Peter's doing his *Evil Dead* routine. Just FYI, I've told him many times that it's not funny."

Natalie nudged Sarah with her elbow, then jerked her chin in the direction of the hee-hawing boys. "It's like Peter's known all of them forever," she said quietly.

"It's just like when Brynn and I were working on the movie. Peter was always coming up with fun stuff for everybody to do," Sarah answered. "He even got some of the stars to hang with us. Everybody liked the guy."

"You weren't the only one he fooled," Natalie commented. "He made everybody think he was this fun, nice person."

"I'm the only one who thought he had a crush on them, though," Sarah said. She turned away, like it was too painful to look at Peter laughing it up at the next table.

Natalie decided it was time for a subject change. "What do you think we'll be doing tonight?" she asked.

"Ellie likes crafty stuff, so probably something with paint or glue guns or clay," Chelsea answered.

"I actually saw her with a stack of football jerseys.

She said we could decorate them for the game," Sarah added.

"Jackson will probably come up with something sporty," Avery said. "Like an indoor obstacle course."

"Avery knows all about Jackson." Jenna winked. "Stalkers always know all about their victims."

"I never stalked him," Avery protested. "I just had a teeny crushlet."

"I want to play charades tonight," Brynn volunteered.

"Of course you do, Drama Queen," Priya joked.

"Whatever we play, I want the teams to be boys against girls," Sarah said. "I seriously feel the need to kick some boy butt."

Natalie took another look at the next table over. The guys—including Peter—were all laughing and talking at once. She noticed a couple of them now had spaghetti sauce smeared on their ears. Were they actually imitating Peter? That so wasn't right.

"Your brother seems to be making friends fast," Jenna commented to Avery.

Avery raised her eyebrows. "Yeah, he does. Huh. At home, all he does is lock himself in his room and watch old movies. It's like he pretends he has his own apartment, and the rest of us are just his annoying neighbors."

"Even the new baby?" Priya asked. "How could he ignore somebody so cute? Those pictures you posted on the blog were adorable."

"I just took some new ones. I'm making a calendar for my parents. Whenever they're out, I do a stealth photo session. I just took a bunch with her dressed as the perfect chubby little cupid. And, to answer your question, most of the time Peter ignores her, too."

Natalie was only half listening. She kept looking over at Peter. The only reason he was fitting in so well was because the rest of the guys had no idea what he was really like.

And she was going to do something about it, she decided as she saw Peter and Jackson get up and head over to the buffet table to get seconds. "Come with me," she said to Sarah, then got up and strode over to the boys' table.

"Hey, Nat," Miles said. "And Sarah," he added, noticing her standing behind Natalie.

"So you've met Peter," Natalie commented.

"Yeah, he's really funny," David told her.

"No, no he's not," Natalie answered. "He isn't at all funny. And he isn't somebody you guys should hang out with."

"Why? Is he a zombie or something?" Ben joked.

"You don't have to worry about it if he is," Justin told him. "They feed on brains, so you're safe."

"Neither of you are funny, either," Natalie told him.

"Somebody get Nat a dictionary," David suggested. "She's unclear on the meaning of the word 'funny.'"

"Look, Natalie's right. Ch— I mean, Peter is pretty uncool," Sarah added.

"Brain-eating zombie uncool or he-didn't-notice-my-new-haircut uncool?" Ben asked. "Because with girls, the hair thing can be a huge deal. But guys don't really care if their friends don't notice stuff like that."

"How do you even know him, anyway?" Justin said.

"I met him this summer. Nat and Brynn, too," Sarah answered.

"Uh, excuse me," Peter said, walking up to Natalie. "That's my chair."

Natalie didn't move at first. Instead, she gave Peter a long, cool glance. "Sorry," she said. She moved back a few steps and turned to Sarah. "You'll notice I know how to apologize."

"Did you, um, want something?" Peter asked, talking more to his plate than either Natalie or Sarah.

"We just wanted to make sure these guys are treating you the way you *deserve* to be treated," Natalie answered, and stormed off.

chapter

FOUR

Avery, Natalie, Sarah, and Jenna were next up for s'more making. They took their seats in front of the massive fireplace and started on the marshmallow-roasting part of the process. Avery liked her marshmallows a perfect, even, golden brown, like a first-week-of-summer suntan.

She was tempted to ask Natalie and Sarah what had gone down at the boys' table in the dining room. Avery had seen the Look of Death Natalie had given Peter. But she decided she wasn't going to go there. She'd given her brother her advice on how to handle the situation, and now she was staying out of it.

"I went to this restaurant in New York where they brought out a little flame pot so everyone could cook s'mores," Natalie commented. The look she had trained on her marshmallow was the opposite of the one she'd given Peter, a complete Look of Love.

"There's just something wrong about that," Jenna commented. "S'mores need to have that taste of wood smoke." Her marshmallow melted off its stick and plopped to the bottom of the fire.

"Or ashes," Sarah joked, as Jenna attempted to rescue the blackening marshmallow using two sticks as pinchers. All that happened was that the sticks caught fire.

"So, Ave, you're an old-time Walla Walla camper," Jenna said. "What's the scoop on the football game?" She stuck a fresh marshmallow on a fresh stick.

"I want to hear this, too." Priya squeezed into a spot between Jenna and Avery.

"There's been a game between the Walla Walla girls and the Talamini girls every year for about the last fifty," Avery explained. "Camp Talamini always has their reunion over Presidents' Weekend, too. They stay at a lodge a few miles away from this one."

"And Walla Walla girls always kick behind, am I right?" Jenna asked.

"I wouldn't exactly say that," Avery admitted. "The last four years, Talamini has won the game, which means they've had the Sports award at their camp all that time. I'd hardly remember what it looks like, except the Talamini campers parade it around the room at the awards ceremony. They practically shake it in our faces."

"I feel a *grrrr* coming on," Jenna informed her friends.

"Me too," Priya agreed. "But, remember, Jenna, Walla Walla has an infusion of sports talent this year. You and me—they've never seen the likes of us. Except for maybe with Sarah. This is our first Walla Walla reunion. That means this year we'll be showing Camp Talamini some new tricks."

"Definitely," Jenna agreed. "I even worked out

some plays. I'll show you when we get back upstairs. We're all suiting up, right?"

"That's jock talk for playing," Sarah told Avery and Natalie.

Avery put down the square of chocolate she'd just picked up. "Do you see these nails?" She turned her right hand back and forth, doing the Miss America wave. "Do these look like the hands of a football player?"

"They look very much like my nails. Which means, no, they don't," Natalie answered. She reached over and ran a finger along the back of Avery's hand. "You got a paraffin wax treatment with the manicure, am I right?"

"I'm not going to ask what that is. Because I have no interest in the answer," Jenna joked. "Besides, let's get back to the real issue. You two are going to be on the team, right?"

"It's going to be a historic year," Priya coaxed. "The year we regain what is rightfully ours—this trophy we've never seen, but desperately, desperately want!" Priya's eyes shone at the thought.

"I'll think about it," Avery answered. "But you athletic types would have to give me some private coaching. I've managed to avoid any contact with football my whole life."

"We will absolutely teach you," Sarah said. "And we'll even repair your manicure after the game. Not that anything's going to happen to it!"

"What about you, Nat?" Jenna asked.

Natalie wrinkled her nose. Before she could answer, Jackson jogged to the front of the room, clapping to get everyone's attention. *He's very yummy*, Avery couldn't help thinking. She'd gotten over that crush she used to have on the counselor. But that didn't mean it wasn't fun to look.

"Before we start our epic game night, Dr. Steve and I have a movie to show you," Jackson announced.

A movie. That should make Peter happy. Avery glanced over at her brother. He was pretty smiley. Actually, he'd been pretty smiley at dinner. The guys were treating him as if they'd been hanging out together for lots of camp summers.

Jackson killed the lights. A movie—kind of grainy and scratchy—appeared on the screen. "Look at that hair!" Natalie exclaimed.

Avery's eyes had gone directly to the hair, too. "A mullet?" she exclaimed. "Did girls actually wear mullets?"

"Ave, the cheerleaders are *guys*," Jenna pointed out. "The one on the far left obviously didn't bother with a wig." The rest of the cheer guys wore wigs, mostly long and straight, but a few had wigs with insanely elaborate '80s-style feathering.

"I wasn't looking at him. I was looking at her. The girl running after the girl with the ball," Avery answered. "I swear she has a mullet."

"Back in the day—by which I mean the '80s—the mullet was an equal opportunity hairstyle," Dr. Steve called out.

"Business in the front, party in the back!" Justin exclaimed. "That's what my uncle says about his. He's been proudly wearing the mullet for twenty years. I'm thinking of getting him a T-shirt that says so."

"This is footage from the very first Walla Walla powder-puff game," Dr. Steve interrupted the mullet-talk. "Sadly, it was also the very first time we lost to Camp Talamini."

A loud chorus of boos followed that comment. "Easy, easy," Dr. Steve told the group. "I should have said, it was the first year we lost the game. But the Walla Walla guys did bring home the Spirit award."

"The camp with the best boy cheerleaders gets an award, too. And Talamini has taken that one home the last four years, too," Avery explained to her friends.

A new game appeared on-screen. "That's some big hair," Jenna commented.

It was true. The wigs on the guy cheerleaders and the hair on the girls on the field was just *big*. Like they'd used every kind of volume-enhancing product on the market at once.

"Here's another game from the eighties," Dr. Steve said. "Walla Walla triumphed—in Sport and Spirit."

A few moments of a couple more games—each with slightly different hairstyles and cheerleading outfits—appeared on-screen. "Okay, these next games are important," Jackson said. "These are clips from the last four games we lost to Talamini. We lost the last four Spirit awards, too."

"Why are you torturing us with this?" David moaned aloud.

"It's not for torture, it's for motivation," Jackson answered. "If Talamini wins this weekend, it will be a five-year streak for them. And that would break the record for the number of consecutive games either camp has won."

"Are we going to let that happen?" Dr. Steve yelled.

"No!" Avery and the other campers shouted.

"I can't hear you. ARE WE GOING TO LET THAT HAPPEN?" Jackson screamed, pumping both fists in the air.

"NOOOOO!" they shouted back, and the screen faded to black.

Jackson hit the lights. "So who is going to lead the powder-puff team to victory?" he called. "We need a captain."

"Me!" Jenna jumped to her feet.

Sarah was right there with her. "I will!"

Jackson laughed. "Love the enthusiasm."

"And we need all the enthusiasm we can get. Sarah and Jenna—you're co-captains," Dr. Steve announced. Grinning, Sarah and Jenna slapped hands.

"Okay, who's going to be on the team?" Jenna asked.

"I'm in!" Priya answered.

Of course. Priya was one of the sporty girls. Unlike Avery.

Brynn and several other girls raised their hands. Natalie wasn't one of them. That made sense. Avery and Natalie were alike in their general lack of interest in running around, sweating, and getting dirty. To her surprise, Chelsea volunteered. Chelsea was usually with Avery and Nat when it came to staying pretty.

"Avery, you've been a Walla Walla girl forever," Sarah said. "Lots longer than me or Jenna. You want to be in on smashing Talamini and making Walla Walla number one again. I know you do!"

"Av-er-y, Av-er-y, Av-er-y," Jenna began to chant. All Avery's friends began to join in.

Avery looked down at her beautiful nails with their slate gray polish. She sighed. Then she said, "I've never even played football. But if Walla Walla needs me, I'm there."

▲ ▲ ▲

"How about Rabid Poodles?" Brynn suggested. "We could make poodles out of the black glitter. That would look good on the shirts."

Natalie studied the pile of jerseys in the center of the table. Black would look good against the bright yellow. She scanned the tubes of puffy paint, bottles of glitter, piles of ribbon, and other T-shirt decorating supplies scattered in front of them.

"Why are all the ideas so girly?" Jenna complained.

"Um, because we're girls," Sloan offered.

"Did you not hear the *rabid* part?" Brynn asked.

"I like the idea of a girly name," Sarah said. "I mean, it's called powder-puff football. Nothing girlier than that. I think we should come up with the softest, sweetest, powder-puffiest name we can. Then we'll go out there and kick butt."

Jenna smiled. "So it would be kind of like camouflage—the girly name?"

"Yeah," Sarah answered. "And we'll decorate the shirts as girly as we can, too." She turned to Natalie. "Are you sure you won't join the team? It's going to be so fun."

Natalie ran her tongue over her braces. "The

cheerleaders are going to need some cheerers to lead," she answered. "I will scream my throat bloody for you."

Actually, that gave her an idea for a way for her to bring a trophy home to Walla Walla without getting all cold and muddy in the process. While Natalie had gotten to actually enjoy some sports, she drew the line at the cold and muddy ones.

Natalie stood up. "I have something I need to talk to Dr. Steve about," she told her friends. She hurried out of the dining room and into the main room and almost got slammed by a chain of people playing elbow tag. She dodged and weaved her way over to Dr. Steve and Jackson, who were hanging out near the Foosball table.

"I'd like to volunteer my services as cheerleading coach," she told them.

Dr. Steve raised his eyebrows. "Interesting idea."

"We want to win the Spirit trophy, too," Natalie reminded them. "And for that, I think the guys are going to need some assistance. I know lots of routines. Plus the wigs you dug up—they need some intensive styling."

"I say go for it," Jackson said. Dr. Steve nodded.

"Why don't you get yourself a partner?" Dr. Steve suggested. "We have co-captains for the football team. Let's have co-coaches for the cheerleaders."

"I'll get right on it!" Natalie told them and hurried away.

Hmmm. Who would be good working with the guys? she wondered to herself. Brynn, because she was all about voice projection and knew about dance and performing. But Brynn was on the team. She wouldn't have time to do both.

Avery would also be great. Avery had a knack for getting people to do what she wanted, and Natalie figured that would include winning the Spirit trophy. But weirdly, Avery had decided to join the team, too.

As she ran through a mental list of all the campers, she noticed Joanna over in a corner, reading. It wasn't like Joanna to go off by herself when all her friends were around. Nat remembered how quiet Joanna had been at dinner. She'd said nothing was wrong, but it looked like she could use some cheering up.

Natalie headed over to her. Joanna put her book aside once she saw Natalie approaching. It was a volume of the encyclopedia from the big bookshelf behind her. "Do you have a big report for school coming up?" she asked.

"No. It's just something I wanted to find out more about," Joanna said.

"Good. If it was for school, I should probably leave you alone. But since it's not—want to help me teach the guys how to be cheerleaders?"

Joanna hesitated. "Come on. It'll be fu-un," Natalie promised.

"Okay. Sure." Joanna stood up.

"What kind of routine do you think we should have them do? Something athletic—with gymnastics moves, maybe? Or something with lots of dance moves?" Natalie suggested.

"Either would be okay, I guess," Joanna answered.

"I guess we should see what kind of skills they all have," Natalie said. "Ben's a good dancer, I know. Miles isn't bad. I don't know if any of them have tried gymnastics." Natalie scanned the room. "So who should we recruit first?"

Joanna gave a little shrug. "Any of them."

This co-coach arrangement wasn't feeling very co-. But, whatever, Natalie could handle things if Joanna didn't want to get that involved. Again, Natalie wondered what was going on with her friend. There was definitely something off with her.

"Connor's over by the cookies. Let's hit him first. Connor's usually up for almost anything." Plus he was a good friend. Natalie led the way toward the refreshments, then veered sharply when she saw Peter heading there, too. She wasn't ready to deal with Peter right now.

"Um, actually, let's ask Justin first. Cheerleading's really athletic, and Justin is all about the sports. Every summer he's been captain of either the soccer or the baseball team, and he does those amazing dives off the high dive," Natalie said. "Justin!" she called. "We need you."

Justin broke away from the tag game. "What's up?" he asked when he reached them.

Natalie waited a moment to give Joanna the chance to tell him. She didn't, so Natalie jumped in. "We're recruiting cheerleaders. And we want you!"

Justin backed up a step. "Whoa. I am not putting on a skirt," he told her.

"Don't you want Walla Walla to win the Spirit trophy?" Natalie demanded.

"Yeah. Of course," Justin answered. "But I am not putting on a skirt."

"Fine," Natalie told him, exasperated. She spotted David playing the pretty kitty game with a group of people. In the game, one person was a cat. The cat went up to someone in the circle, and the person had to say "pretty kitty" three times in a row without laughing. If they cracked up, they were out.

Brynn had left the shirt-designing group and was playing the cat. She stopped in front of David and rubbed her head against his knee, meowing.

And David laughed. Nat had known he would. David couldn't stay serious for more than a few seconds at a time, even when there wasn't a girl meowing at him. Which made him the perfect choice for her cheerleading squad. David wouldn't freak out at the idea of wearing a skirt. He'd think it was funny.

Natalie walked over to him, Joanna trailing behind her, and gave him the pitch. Being a cheerleader would bring glory—and a trophy—to Walla Walla. And it would be fun.

David agreed. Of course. That boy sure loved his fun.

Brynn was on a roll. She knocked Miles out of the game before he could get even one "pretty kitty" out. Natalie waved him over to the group. "Miles, how would you like to help bring the Spirit trophy home to Walla Walla where it belongs?"

"I'm doing it," David said.

"Yeah, David's doing it," Natalie repeated. Joanna nodded.

"David doing something doesn't mean it's a good idea," Miles answered. "In fact, a lot of times David doing something means it's a bad, bad, getting-in-trouble idea."

Like Miles ever worried about getting in trouble. But he might be worried about performing in front of a bunch of people. He avoided camp drama productions, and Natalie was pretty sure he only mouthed the words during camp sing-alongs.

"There's no way you'll get in trouble for being a cheerleader. It's a completely Dr. Steve approved activity," Natalie told him. "And it'll be fu-un."

"Let me think about it," Miles answered.

The way he said it—and the glimmer of fear in his eyes—made it clear that after he thought about it, he was going to say no.

Winning the Spirit trophy was going to be harder than Natalie thought. How was she supposed to produce an awesome cheerleading squad without cheerleaders?

chapter
FIVE

"I would rather clean the bathrooms with a toothbrush than put on a cheerleading skirt," Justin said.

"What's your problem? It's a goof. It'll be fun," David answered.

"So you said yes?" Peter asked. The room he shared with David, Ben, and Justin had turned into hangout central. A bunch of the other guys had ended up there after the official camp activities were done for the night.

"Of course," David said. "Nat's cool. Who says no to Nat?"

Peter hadn't had the chance to say no since Natalie hadn't asked him. Which was good. His plan to avoid her and Sarah wouldn't work very well if he was on her cheer squad.

Miles's hand shot up. "Me. I said no."

David snorted. "You did not. I was standing right next to you. You said you'd think about it."

"Okay, okay, I haven't actually gotten to the saying no part. Because saying no to Nat when she's looking at you with her big blue eyes is sort of hard. But tomorrow I'm going to change my 'maybe' to an 'absolutely not.' No matter what, me, in front of a bunch of people— not going to happen." He ran his fingers through his hair. "Although maybe I'll tell Joanna. Because of the saying no to Natalie problem."

"I had no problem saying no to her," Justin volunteered.

So she asked him, too, Peter thought. That was Justin, Miles, and David.

"Wuss. I'm putting on a skirt to cheer for Brynn," Ben said.

"That's because you're a big hambone, not because you're being supportive of Brynn," Connor joked.

Ben laughed. "I am sort of hammy. But you know what—ham is gooood."

"What about you, Connor?" Peter asked.

"No way," Connor said quickly. "Nat's great and all. But nobody's great enough to convince me to rah-rah."

So she asked Connor, too, Peter thought. Had she asked every single guy except him? Not that he wanted her to ask. But if he was the only one left out, that wasn't exactly fair.

Like what you did to Sarah was fair, he thought. And after talking to Avery, he knew Natalie felt like he'd done exactly the same thing to her.

"There *are* guy cheerleaders, you know," Ben commented. "Some of them do backflips and all this other awesome gymnastic stuff."

"I'm into the gymnastic part. But only if I can wear pants," Justin said.

"They do lifts with the girls. That's pretty cool," Ben added.

"But the girls are going to be us," Connor reminded him.

"Another reason I'm absolutely, definitely saying no first thing tomorrow," Miles responded.

"Forget about tomorrow. Let's talk about what we're doing tonight," David said.

"I was thinking about doing that thing where you lay really still and close your eyes for about eight hours," Ben joked. "But if you have something better in mind . . ."

"Come on, Ben. This is a camp Walla Walla event. We can't forget that. And what do we do every time we're at camp?" David asked.

"Prank the girls," Justin answered.

"Ding, ding, ding! We have a winner!" David exclaimed.

"What do you have in mind?" Connor asked.

"If I'm wearing a cheerleading outfit, I want to fill it out," David said. "That means I need to stuff. And that means I need something *to* stuff."

"You want to do a raid for bras?" Justin shook his head admiringly. "That's bold, my friend."

"So you're in?" David asked him.

Justin grinned. "I'm *so* in."

"What about the rest of you?" David glanced around the room.

All the guys were smiling and nodding. *Uh-oh*, Peter thought. This was not good. His plan was to stay away from Natalie and Sarah. Pulling a prank on them—and the other girls—was in direct opposition to the plan. Not that he could tell the guys that. Telling them about the avoidance plan would mean explaining why there had to be a plan in the first place. Peter didn't want to go there.

"What about *Evil Dead* 2?" Peter blurted out. He thought he sounded a little desperate and told himself to calm down. "Uh, didn't you guys want to watch it? We could do that tonight."

"Supremely cool movie," Ben said.

"We can do both," Justin said. "We can't pull off a raid until we're sure the girls are asleep. We watch the movie, then we make our move."

Abort, abort, Peter's brain began chanting. He couldn't, though. Everyone was already on the *Evil Dead* and Bra train. There was no way to stop it.

Peter set up his portable DVD player on the end of one of the beds, so they could all sit in front of it, and popped in the movie. For the first time, it didn't make him laugh. Not even the Three Stooges-esque scene where Bruce Campbell broke all those plates over his own head.

The other guys cracked up. A couple of them had to press pillows against their mouths so they wouldn't laugh so loud that one of the counselors would come in to check up on them.

All too soon, the movie was over. David divided the guys into teams and assigned each team a room to raid. Peter got assigned to the room that Natalie was in. Of course.

Peter had to at least try and stop it. He'd probably

get flattened by the train, but he had to make the attempt. "Look, I know I'm the new guy," he said. "I don't know what kind of pranks you usually pull. But maybe we should do something like put Tabasco sauce in the pancake batter. Girls are sensitive about their underwear. I know. I have a sister."

"A prank isn't a prank if there isn't some shouting or crying from the prankees," David pronounced. "Well, maybe not crying. But who would cry over underwear, no matter how sensitive they are? Besides, we need the bras for cheerleading."

"I don't know what Natalie and Sarah's problem with you is," Justin told Peter. "You're way nicer than the rest of us."

I knew it, Peter thought. *Natalie and Sarah were talking to the guys about me. But they clearly didn't give out many details.*

"Don't worry about it, Peter," David said. "This prank isn't any worse than other things we've done. Okay, Team One—go!"

Team One. That was Peter's team. Reluctantly, he followed Ben and Miles out of the room and down the dark hallway. Ben signaled for them to stop when they reached their assigned room. He pressed his ear against the door, listening hard. Satisfied, Ben eased the door open. He pointed at Peter, then at a tall dresser, then signaled that he and Miles would take the closet.

Nobody wake up, Peter thought as he crept over to the dresser. He slowly slid open the top drawer. It was jammed full of clothes. But there was no underwear on top and he didn't want to start pawing. He opened the next drawer. Sweaters on top. He'd have to go deeper. He glanced behind him at the row of beds. It looked like all the girls were still sleeping. Peter slid his hand under the sweaters, fishing around for something that felt right.

His fingers grazed something soft. Silky. He pulled the item free. Score. A lavender bra with a tiny bow in the center. He hoped David—or whoever—would be very happy stuffing it for cheerleading.

Peter shut the drawer, then did another bed check. *Click!*

He winced as a beam of light hit him right in the eyes. He winced again as someone let out a long, loud scream of fury.

Peter blinked a few times, enough to make out that it was Natalie holding the flashlight and doing the screaming.

"Is that my bra you're holding?" she shouted.

▲ ▲ ▲

"Do you think the boys aren't getting breakfast as punishment for the raid?" Brynn asked, looking over at the empty table next to theirs.

"That's not Dr. Steve's usual style," Sarah commented, spearing a piece of apple pancake.

"I hope he comes up with something really terrible," Natalie said. "They deserve it!"

"It was a prank, Nat. It's not like we haven't pulled some ourselves," Jenna told her.

"It wasn't just a prank," Natalie insisted. "It was disrespectful. It was embarrassing. It was just . . . wrong."

"O-kay," Jenna said, looking surprised.

Belatedly, Natalie realized she'd been thinking a lot more about Peter using her to get to her dad—well, using Sarah, which was the same thing—than about the boys' raid.

"Has anyone heard a weather report?" Joanna asked, yawning. She looked as if she hadn't gotten much sleep last night. *Probably because of the boys*, Natalie thought. *Joanna probably had a hard time falling asleep after all the uproar.* Natalie certainly had. She'd laid in her bed for hours, staring at the ceiling and seething. Which was probably also a lot more about Peter's past behavior than any prank, she realized.

"Here come the guys!" Priya exclaimed before anyone could answer Joanna. "Doing the walk of shame!"

Peter did look embarrassed, Natalie noticed. A couple of the other guys, too. But David was smirking, and it looked like Ben was trying not to laugh.

Dr. Steve strode to the front of the room. "Can I get your attention for a minute?" he called. "First, good morning."

"Good morning, Dr. Steve!" Natalie and the rest of the campers called back.

"As most of you probably heard, there was some commotion on the girls' wing last night," Dr. Steve continued.

"It sounded like *Saw VIII* was being filmed over there," one of the older guys joked.

"Nothing quite so dramatic," Dr. Steve replied. "But there was a prank pulled, and I've just had a conference with the perpetrators."

"Uh-oh," somebody muttered.

"I'd heard that Natalie and Joanna were having trouble getting cheerleaders, so I discussed this with the boys in question. We decided that all the boys involved would join the cheerleading squad to make things up to the girls." Dr. Steve smiled. "And to have some fun and get Walla Walla that Spirit trophy."

The girls—and the guys who weren't involved—hooted and applauded. Natalie looked over at the boys who had taken part in the raid. David and Ben were cracking up, probably because they'd already signed on to be cheerleaders in the first place. The other guys didn't look happy. Miles looked a little nauseous, and Peter looked like he'd been sentenced to a prison term. Natalie couldn't believe the guys' reactions. Like showing a little camp spirit was *that bad*!

"Natalie and Joanna—when do you want your recruits to show up for practice?" Dr. Steve asked.

Natalie glanced at Joanna. It was clear Joanna was expecting her to answer. "Right after breakfast. Main room," Natalie announced. "Be ready to work!"

Natalie bolted down her breakfast, which didn't help smooth out the nervous knots in her stomach. Suddenly, Natalie was so concerned about leading the boys to a Spirit Award victory that she didn't have time to feel enraged toward Peter. If only she could have a little prep time before the cheer meeting. She'd been thinking about routines, but she still didn't feel quite ready.

Nat looked over at Joanna again. Joanna wasn't

anywhere near finished with her breakfast. In fact, it looked like she'd taken three bites—tops. Natalie didn't have time to wait for her. She stood up. "See you in there, Joanna," she said.

"Good luck!" Brynn called as Natalie started out of the room.

"I'm afraid you're going to need it," Jenna added cheerfully. Why shouldn't she be cheerful? Everyone on the football team was there voluntarily.

Okay, Natalie thought as she walked into the main room. *Where to start? Basic moves*, she decided. *With spectacular technique.*

Some of the campers had been using an easel with a large pad of paper to play Pictionary the night before. Natalie pulled the easel away from the wall and started drawing stick figures that illustrated the moves she wanted the guys to learn first.

"Don't tell me. I got it." Natalie turned and saw Ben leading the pack of guys into the room. "It's a . . . actually, I don't got it," Ben admitted.

"It's a cheerleader doing a move called the 'Left K,'" Natalie told him.

Jordan raised his hand. Natalie nodded her head, smiling. "Yes?"

"Will this be on the test?" he asked.

"Everything's going to be on the test," Natalie answered. "Right, Joanna?" she added as she spotted her friend come into the room.

"What?" Joanna asked. "Oh, yeah, right. On the test," she quickly added as she joined Natalie at the front of the room. "I had that delayed understanding thing. You know, when you hear something, but don't actually understand it until a few seconds later, when you've already said 'what'?"

Natalie thought those were the most words she'd heard Joanna say in a row since they arrived at the lodge yesterday.

"Okay, I want you all in a straight line." Natalie gestured to the open space in front of her. She tried to keep her eyes off Peter. It was easier to pretend he wasn't there if she didn't look at him.

"Uh, could you draw that for us?" Justin asked.

Natalie narrowed her eyes at him.

"Seriously. I ingested a huge amount of additives and preservatives last night. Forget about artificial colors. The punch at dinner was blue, remember," Justin added. "All that stuff has to have destroyed my brain, just the way my parents always said it would. So, straight line? Can you put it on the board?"

"Doing badly at practice, pretending you can't learn moves, any of that—it won't get you kicked off the squad," Natalie warned the guys "It'll just get you more practice."

Joanna didn't say anything. *Thanks for the backup*, Natalie thought.

After the boys arranged themselves in a ragged line, Natalie pulled in a deep breath. *Get them motivated first*, she told herself. "I know most of you don't want to be here. But we're going to have fun. Cheerleading is actually as much of a sport as football. You need the same skills. Coordination. Strength—"

"The pom-poms are that heavy?" David interrupted.

"I need info on the skirts before we go any further," Connor said. "Are they going to make my butt look big?"

Miles gave a high, long laugh. A nervous laugh. The rest of the guys joined in. Natalie was still trying not to look at Peter, but she caught him laughing, too. Or maybe he was just smiling.

"If you guys want to goof around all day, I can't stop you," Natalie snapped. "But if you don't practice— really practice—Walla Walla is going to lose the Spirit trophy for the fifth year in a row. The only way to win is to work at it. Even if you have connections to a famous Dallas Cowboys cheerleader, it doesn't matter. Connections don't mean anything." She hoped Peter realized that last part was a message just for him. "Work does. Talent does."

"Um, maybe we should start working on the first move," Joanna suggested.

Natalie realized she'd been ranting. Well, so what? There was one cheerleader in front of her who needed to know exactly how she felt about people using people just to get the inside track. People did that to her all the time. They all thought, "Oh, I know! I'll be nice to Tad Maxwell's daughter. Then she'll tell her dad to give me a job."

She gave up trying to avoid looking at Peter. She glared at him full-on. But he wouldn't meet her gaze. Wimp.

"I have a question," David said.

At least David had volunteered to be here. "Yes?" Natalie said.

"If I wanted to meet a Dallas Cowboys cheerleader, how would I do that? Do you have a phone number I could—"

"Shut it!" Natalie cut him off. "Please," she added.

Why had she thought this was a good idea? These guys were never going to listen to her. They were just going to try to top one another by making stupid jokes.

Natalie jerked her chin up. She wasn't going to let that happen. She was going to get the squad in perfect shape and win that trophy, even if it killed her. Or them.

Forget motivation. She was going to make them work. She pointed to the top figure on the chart. "Let's start here."

chapter SIX

"What do the Sweet Lil' Kitties say?" Jenna and Sarah shouted.

"Rrrroar!" most of the girls yelled.

"Meow," Avery joked. Chelsea winked at her. The two of them weren't exactly football-player types.

"I'm going to ask you that again after practice!" Jenna told Avery. "Here's what we have planned, team. This morning it's all about skills, skills, skills."

"We have stations set up all over the field," Sarah continued. "Tackling." She pointed to three lumpy dummies on wheels. "Passing and catching." She pointed to the middle of the field. "And kicking," she pointed to the side of the field opposite the dummies.

"Tackling?" Molly asked. "They don't let us play tackle at my school's powder-puff games."

"You don't think a team called the Sweet Lil' Kitties plays touch, do you?" Jenna answered.

"Rrrroar!" Priya called out, along with Shawn and a couple other girls.

"Powder-puff is changing," Sarah added. "We got the okay to tackle as long as we all wear pads." She nodded to a pile of equipment next to her. "Jackson hooked us up. He got the local high school to loan us the dummies, too."

"Are we wearing pads for practice?" Priya asked.

"You might want to wear them for the whole thing, but definitely when you're working with the dummies," Sarah said.

Avery was definitely wearing them all the time. No bruises for her. Not attractive.

"Let's get started," Sarah continued. "Three of you over at the tackling station. The rest divide up between the kicking station and the passing and throwing station. Jenna and I will be around to give you tips. Ellie's going to help out, too."

Ellie waved to the group. "This is Walla Walla's year!" she exclaimed. "I can feel it."

"Me too! And you know me and my feelings!" Sloan exclaimed. She'd decided to be an alternate player for the team, but mostly help out with equipment and scorekeeping. "I'm going to go make hot chocolate for your first break!" she added.

Avery caught Sloan shooting a concerned glance at the sky as she started back toward the lodge. Avery looked up, too. The sky was an amazing blue that looked freshly washed and polished. Right now it didn't seem like they were in danger of that snowstorm Sloan's aunt had been predicting.

"Ave, looks like you're up with the dummies," Jenna told her, and Avery realized that she was the only who hadn't chosen a skill station.

Avery wrinkled her nose as she used two fingers to

pull out a couple of the kneepads from the pile Sloan had made. She didn't know what color the pad had been originally, but now it was a dingy gray. Lovely. *You're longtime Walla Walla,* she told herself. *You've got to support your camp.*

She geared up and trotted over to the row of dummies. Priya let out a yell, then charged one. She slammed it with her shoulder and it slid back a few feet.

"Cool!" Avery shouted. *But kinda painful looking,* she thought.

Brynn eyed the next dummy. "I'm taking you downtown!" she bellowed. She ran at the dummy, but hesitated a fraction of a second just before she reached it. The dummy hardly moved when her shoulder hit it.

Guess it's my turn, Avery thought. She studied the dummy. Priya had hit it a little lower than Brynn. She'd also been moving faster. But it made sense that it mattered where you hit. She figured the lower the better.

She took a step forward, then hesitated a bit. Thinking about hitting something in theory was different than *actually* hitting it.

"Try pretending it's someone that makes you mad!" Jenna called, heading their way.

Okay, who makes me mad? Avery asked herself. Lady Gaga's fashion choices, for one. Avery got that Lady Gaga was trying to look out-there. But still . . .

She imagined the dummy was Lady Gaga, then hurled herself at it. She kept her shoulder low, aiming for the knees. *Thunk!* It did hurt a little when she body-slammed the dummy. But it felt really good when her dummy slid back past Priya's. Priya—who was all sporty.

"Way to go, Avery!" Priya exclaimed. Brynn clapped and Jenna gave the Kitties' roar.

Hmmm. Maybe I've just discovered something else I excel at, Avery thought, pride welling up in her chest. Suddenly, she couldn't wait for Monday's game.

▲ ▲ ▲

That afternoon, Sloan stood in front of the window in the bedroom she shared with Natalie, Joanna, and Jenna. It was only four o'clock, but the sky was already dark with gray clouds. Soft, fluffy snowflakes were falling. They looked so beautiful in the light spilling from the lodge's window.

But, beautiful as they were, Sloan couldn't help feeling sad as she watched the flakes. Sad because in the front drive there were three cars waiting for campers, campers with nervous parents who had decided they had to leave the reunion early.

Were those parents right? Was Sloan's aunt right? Was there going to be an enormous snowstorm? Would Dr. Steve decide to shut down the reunion and make everyone leave? Sloan had to fight, and beg, and plead, and spout statistics to get here. Was she going to have to go home *now*, when she was having so much fun?

Don't get ahead of yourself, she thought. The campers who were leaving were all younger than Sloan and her friends. It made sense that their parents were worried about them. If Sloan had been in the fourth or fifth grade like those other campers, her parents wouldn't have given permission for her to come to the reunion, no matter what arguments she came up with.

Joanna stepped up beside her. "Do you think Dr. Steve will send us all home?" she asked, echoing Sloan's worries. Joanna didn't sound worried, though. She sounded . . . almost hopeful.

"It's not snowing very hard," Sloan answered.

"But the flakes are coming down thicker," Joanna pointed out. "I think it's getting worse."

Sloan studied the snow. She didn't think the flakes were falling any faster than they had been. She'd still call what was happening out there a light snow.

Natalie crowded up next to them. "We better not get sent home," she said. "That would be like the boys winning."

"The boys don't want to go home," Sloan protested.

"The boys don't want to be cheerleaders. If they get to go home, they get out of it. That means they win. And they aren't winning," Natalie answered. "I'm winning."

"My team—Sarah's and mine—is winning, too, unless the game gets called off. So, snow, snow, go away. Come again when I can have a snow day and can stay home from school and play," Jenna improvised, laughing at herself.

"So, to recap, we're all winning," Sloan said.

There was a quick double tap on the door. "Come in!" Jenna and Sloan called together.

Dr. Steve stepped inside. "I thought I'd give a snow report in each room," he said. "With some campers leaving, I suspect there might be questions for me."

"Are we going to have to go home?" Sloan cried.

Dr. Steve laughed. "Questions like that," he answered. "I just checked the weather report. We're at code orange, which basically means there's a possibility we'll get a severe storm warning. If that happens, I'm afraid we will have to evacuate."

"But we have the blankets, and the wood—" Sloan suddenly realized she sounded like a little girl who'd been told she couldn't have another cookie. "I mean, you said we were prepared for anything."

"We are," Dr. Steve assured her. "I'm a strong believer in preparation. I'm also a strong believer in caution. If a severe storm warning is issued for our area, we're putting the tire chains on the bus and evacuating. Your parents will be notified where and when to pick you up."

Dr. Steve put his hand on Sloan's shoulder. "You're one of several kids who flew in. Don't worry, Sloan. I'm not going to just drop you off at the airport. I'll put you on the plane myself, and if the plane's canceled, you'll stay with my family until the airport is open again. Anyone who can't get home will stay with us."

That might even be kinda fun, Sloan thought. *Or at least better than going home.* Dr. Steve would make sure the campers staying with his family had a good time. But it wasn't hanging with her girls. And that meant it wasn't a reunion.

Dr. Steve must have noticed how upset she was. "No one's evacuating yet," he told her and the other girls. "We're just in wait and see mode." He leaned forward and looked out the window. "So far it doesn't look too severe out there to me!" He gave them a wave and left.

"You said your aunt is a weather nut," Joanna said, still staring out the window. "How often is she wrong?"

"Oh, she's definitely been wrong," Sloan answered. *But not often*, she added to herself. *Not often at all.*

Be wrong just this one time, Aunt Willow, she silently pleaded. *You and the birds and the bears and the wind patterns. Be wrong.*

▲ ▲ ▲

Peter stared out the window at the falling snow. Ben, Justin, and David lounged on their beds behind him.

"My arms are actually sore," Ben complained. "From the Ts and the Ls and the left and right Ks."

"Natalie is pitiless," Justin said. "Did you hear her tell me no when I asked for a water break at the afternoon practice? You're not supposed to say no to water. Humans need water to live. My parents are completely pro water."

Maybe Natalie would have a little more pity if you guys actually practiced without goofing off or joking around every five seconds, Peter thought. He'd tried to stay focused on what she was teaching. He didn't want to make her any angrier at him than she already was. But he'd laughed a few times himself.

Peter turned away from the window. He halfway wished they would all have to leave because of a big storm. Yeah, he was having more fun than he'd expected to. The guys were cool, even after Natalie and Sarah had bad-mouthed him. But his plan to avoid the two girls was now impossible. He could still keep away from Sarah, but not Natalie. He'd been in Natalie's face most of the day—with her shooting white-hot hate at him, and that wasn't going to change tomorrow or Monday.

Which meant he'd need a new plan if he wasn't saved by a forced evacuation. He couldn't go on feeling like a complete worm of a guy. Maybe he should be extra, extra nice to Natalie—and Sarah. He still wasn't going to apologize, though. To apologize meant bringing up the badness, and that seemed like a stupid, stupid idea.

"So you think I should go with the *Legend of Zelda* T-shirt or the *Married . . . With Children* one for the dance?" Ben asked, pushing himself to his feet.

"It's winter. It's snowing. It's not T-shirt weather," Justin told him.

"T-shirts are my signature," Ben said. "And don't worry, Mom, I'll wear a hoodie or something, too."

"So what's the deal with dances at camp?" Peter asked.

"Same as any other place," David answered.

"I mean, is it a couples kind of thing? I know some of the guys have girlfriends here. Or does everyone just go?"

"Little of each," Ben said. "I'm going with Brynn."

"Sarah and I aren't *going together*–going together," David told Peter. "But I'm sure I'll dance with her most of the time."

"Justin is flying solo. All the girls will have a shot at

Justin," Justin said. "It's the only fair thing." Ben threw a pillow at him.

"So, uh, is Natalie going with someone?" Peter asked. If he was going to be extra, extra nice to her, he needed to know. That was the only reason he'd asked. If she was going with someone, extra, extra nice was different than if she wasn't. If she wasn't going with someone, asking her to dance might be part of the niceness plan.

"As far as I know, Nat's not going with anyone," David answered.

"Connor is flying sooo-lo," Connor said.

Justin rolled his eyes. "You realize you need skillz for that, right?" he asked Connor.

"Did you just say 'skillz' with a 'z'?" David said. "Because, as a friend, I have to tell you, you can't pull that off."

So Natalie's going to the dance without a date, Peter thought, not really listening to what the guys said after that. *Good.*

Good. Because that would give him a chance to put in a few minutes being extra, extra nice to her.

chapter
SEVEN

Sarah and Natalie stood together near the fireplace, nibbling on gingerbread, waiting for that moment when people at the dance actually started *to* dance.

It's always the same, camp dances or school ones, Natalie thought. *The music starts, and everyone just stands around for a while.* If things didn't get started soon, she'd start dragging people out on the floor.

"Avery at practice today," Sarah said, shaking her head. "You should have seen it. It's one of those things that has to be seen."

"That bad?" Natalie asked, sympathetically.

"That awesome!" Sarah told her. "Priya was great, of course. Brynn threw herself into it—the way Brynn throws herself into everything. I wouldn't say she's the best player, but she's got a lot of energy!" She paused to take a drink of her hot apple cider. "How was your practice?"

"It was also one of those things that had to be seen," Natalie answered, feeling her shoulders tense up at the memory.

"So, awesome?" Sarah asked.

"Hideous. Just complete hideousness," Natalie said.

"I guess it's different because the girls on the team want to be there," Sarah commented. "Most of the guys are cheerleaders as a punishment. How'd the ones who actually volunteered do?"

Natalie sighed. "You know David and Ben. Nonstop goofing around, as always."

"Want me to say something to David?" Sarah volunteered.

"No. But thanks," Natalie said. "I have to be able to control them by myself."

"Well, you and Joanna," Sarah answered.

"Joanna." Natalie rolled her eyes. "I don't know what's with her. It's like she's a computer in sleep mode or something."

"She has been pretty quiet so far this weekend. Staying by herself a lot." Sarah scanned the room. She tilted her head toward Joanna, who was standing in front of the massive bookcases that lined one wall. "Point made."

"You ready to get this party started?" David asked as he stepped up next to Sarah. He smiled at Natalie, as if he hadn't just spent the day tormenting her.

Sarah gave Natalie an okay-if-I-go look. "Somebody has to get this dance going," Natalie told her and David. "Get out there."

David led the way out to the floor, then started doing the sprinkler. It didn't really go with the music, but it got everyone laughing, and before the song was over, the main room was filled with people dancing.

A couple guys had asked Natalie to dance, but she

just wasn't in the mood. It was Saturday night. The game was on Monday afternoon—camp tradition dictated that it was always on Presidents' Day. How was she going to get her cheerleaders whipped into shape by then? Maybe she and Joanna could do a little routine for them. Or—

"Hi."

The voice pulled Natalie out of her thoughts. Peter stood in front of her. Pretty much the last person she wanted to see right now. Although, after the nightmare that was her cheerleading practice, that list was kind of long.

"Hi, *Chace*," she said.

Peter winced a little. Natalie purposefully used his "stage" name, to remind him of what a poo-head he'd been during the fall. He'd never even bothered to apologize. Now he was standing there like he thought she'd actually want to talk to him. Well, Natalie wasn't playing that. She'd just walk away.

Except before she could, Peter asked her a question. "What's the low T again?" he asked quickly. He was speaking so fast his words ran into each other. "I know the regular T is just arms straight out to the side, but I can't remember the low one. I should have copied down the stick figures. I liked the way you gave them sneakers," he added. "Nice variation."

Natalie raised her eyebrows. "You're complimenting me on my stick figures?"

His face flushed. "I guess I am. You ever have that thing where you start talking and end up saying something you completely didn't plan to?"

"It's good that the stick-figure compliment wasn't part of a planned conversation." Natalie couldn't stop herself from giving a little smile. "A low T is just both hands pressed against your sides."

"Would that be some kind of I?" Peter asked. "Maybe a lowercase one, where your head makes the dot?"

"You could write to the cheerleading board," Natalie suggested.

"I think I will. Because I also think the left K and right Ks don't make sense. A K only goes one way. Everyone knows that," Peter said.

Natalie laughed, then almost clapped both of her hands over her mouth. She shouldn't have been laughing at one of Peter-Chace's jokes.

Except, well . . . she and Sarah and Brynn and Avery had handed down some punishment for his bad behavior. They'd completely embarrassed him in front of the daughter of a director Peter had thought could help his career. Natalie had added some extra punishment of her own, too. Kids of celebrities did occasionally talk. And she had made sure to tell everyone about Peter and his scamming. He was going to have a hard time breaking into the movie business any time soon. And, according to Avery, acting was everything to him, so the punishment—the very deserved punishment—had to have hurt.

Maybe he'd been punished enough. Maybe it would be okay if Natalie eased up on him a little. Just a little.

"Did you have any other cheerleading questions?" Natalie asked.

"I have one, but it's not cheerleading related. Not really, although there is some overlap between the subject and cheerleading," Peter answered.

"Let's hear it," Natalie said.

"Do you want to dance?" Peter asked. She hesitated. "You see the connection, right? Some cheerleading routines are pretty much dancing, right?"

"Pretty weak connection," Natalie told him.

"So is that a no?" Peter asked. His shot-down expression was kind of cute.

"Did you really expect me to say yes?" Easing up on him didn't mean dancing with him. She was standing here talking to him. That was enough.

"I guess not," he admitted. "Unless you thought it would improve my cheering. I know you'd do anything to get the Spirit Award."

"Not anything," she snapped. "You're the one who'd do anything to get what you want, remember?"

Peter held up both hands. "That's fair. I just thought—never mind." He started walking away.

Natalie sighed. "Thought what?"

"I thought maybe I could start making it up to you—for what I did." He laughed, but there wasn't any happiness in the sound. "Stupid, right? Like dancing with me is some great honor you should be grateful for."

"Is that really what you were thinking?" Natalie asked. She'd been scammed before. Not by Peter directly, but by guys just like him. She wasn't going to let it happen again.

"Yeah," Peter admitted. "Like I said, stupid."

"Stupid, but a step in the right direction, I guess," Natalie answered. She studied him for a moment. "You better not be trying another scam now that you know I'm really Tad Maxwell's daughter."

Peter didn't give a big speech to persuade her. He just shook his head and said, "I'm not."

Natalie hesitated, her eyes still on his face, then she took his hand and led him out to a small patch of clear dance floor. Sarah spotted the two of them together and gave Natalie the same look she would have if Natalie were dancing with a python wrapped around her.

Natalie promised herself she'd talk to Sarah later about how Peter had probably been punished enough. Right now, she just wanted to dance, dance, dance, dance, without thinking about anything. It had been a rough day. "Want something to drink?" Peter asked after the song ended.

"Sure," Natalie said. *It's okay*, she told herself. Peter hadn't apologized, true. But he *had* admitted he had something to make up for. And he was very cute. And he was fun. She hadn't expected him to be fun.

Ben and Brynn reached the refreshment table at the same time Natalie and Peter did. Ben grabbed an oatmeal cookie. "You," he said, pointing at Peter. "This guy is hilarious," he told Brynn.

"Have you shown Nat your *Evil Dead* routine?"

Natalie picked up a cup of hot apple cider and wrapped her hands around it. She'd started feeling cold. Guess that snow was getting to her, after all.

Ben grabbed a few paper plates off the table and handed them to Peter. "Do it. It's so insane," he added to Brynn.

Peter started doing a routine. A very planned-out routine. He was acting like his hand was out of his control and that it was hitting him over the head with the plates. Then it was choking him. Then smashing a piece of gingerbread into his forehead.

Ben was laughing so hard he was wheezing. Brynn was cracking up, too. Some people had even stopped dancing to watch.

"Audition over!" Natalie shouted.

Peter instantly dropped the routine and stared at her. "What?"

"Oh, my god." Brynn moved closer to Natalie. "That's what you were doing! It's last fall all over again. Ben said you were cool, but you're exactly the same as we all thought!"

Natalie didn't feel cold anymore. Now she felt like she was going volcanic. Like lava was erupting from her stomach. She hated it when people used her to get to her dad. *Hated* it. And clearly Peter had set this whole thing up. She was sure he'd told Ben to ask him to perform—once it looked like Peter had gotten Natalie all charmed.

"Audition over," Natalie repeated. "And it sucked. Too bad, since you got Tad Maxwell's real daughter to watch you this time."

"Natalie, that's not what—" Peter began.

"Better luck next time, *Chace*." Natalie walked away without looking back.

▲ ▲ ▲

Joanna studied the large bookshelf. She wanted to grab a book to take over next to the fireplace. It was the only warm spot in the room.

She gave a harsh snort of laughter. Somebody had shelved a book on talking to your kids about divorce in the middle of a whole row of romance novels. She didn't want to read any of the romances. Her parents had always told her the story of how they met as one of Joanna's bedtime stories. It was the most romantic story she knew. And the hero and heroine had ended up barely being able to talk to each other.

She definitely didn't want to read the kids and divorce book. She'd lived that story. Her parents had told her that they were still friends and that everything was going to be okay. Lie, and lie. When you were in the hospital, you wanted your friends to visit. When your friend was in the hospital, you went to visit your friend. Which meant her parents absolutely weren't friends. And that everything wasn't even close to okay.

She spotted a big book on home remedies near the bottom shelf and picked it up. Maybe there were some tips in it on how to speed up recovery time after surgery, something that could help her mom.

Joanna sat down in front of the fire and opened the book. She still felt cold. She moved a little closer to the fire. It didn't help. She needed a sweatshirt. She stood and started for the big staircase.

Someone caught her lightly by the arm. Joanna turned and saw Priya smiling at her. "Where ya going?" Priya asked.

"Just up to my room. I want to get my sweatshirt," Joanna answered. "Don't you think it's freezing down here?"

"Actually, no." Priya shoved her dark hair off her face. "I'm starting to sweat. Or glow, as my grandmother calls it. I've been dancing like crazy all night. You don't need a sweatshirt. You just need to get out there!"

"Maybe," Joanna said. But she felt too cold to dance. She felt too cold to do anything. "Maybe later," she added, starting for the stairs again.

"I expect you back down here in two minutes," Priya called after her. "Adding a sweatshirt shouldn't take longer than that. Unless you're Natalie. Or maybe Avery. Or Chelsea."

Joanna waved without looking back at Priya. "I'm serious," Priya added. "I'm timing you."

She's a good friend, Joanna thought. The reunion was filled with good friends. But she still felt lonely somehow.

As she headed up the stairs, Chelsea was on her way down. "The snow has totally stopped!" she announced, pausing in front of Joanna. "There's some wind blowing—I could see the trees moving—but that's it. Is this the big, bad storm? What a joke!"

"Yeah," Joanna answered. "It's cold enough, though!"

"I thought Dr. Steve must have gotten the heater problem fixed. It feels pretty comfy in here to me."

Not me, Joanna thought as she continued up

the stairs, then headed into her room. She pulled a sweatshirt over the T-shirt and sweater she already had on. *Not enough*, she decided. So she pulled a pair of sweats over her jeans. But she still didn't feel warm enough. She decided to crawl under the covers—just for a little while. The dance was almost over, anyway.

She opened the book on home remedies she'd found downstairs, and began reading. She shivered. Maybe she should use her coat as an extra blanket. But that meant getting out of bed. Joanna wrapped the blankets around herself more tightly—and shivered again.

▲ ▲ ▲

Peter lay under the covers with his portable DVD player propped on his chest. He was watching *Elf*, for probably the twenty-seventh time. Which was good, considering he had to watch with the sound off. He'd forgotten to bring his headphones, and all the other guys were sleeping.

Elf usually made him happy, whether he was watching it in the middle of summer, or right at Christmas. If he admitted the truth, he'd viewed it so many times just as much for that happy feeling as to study Will Ferrell's brilliance.

Tonight, though, it wasn't doing it for him. And not because he couldn't hear it. After twenty-seven times, he pretty much had it memorized. Make that he completely had it memorized. A good memory was an important skill for an actor. Although a lot of soap stars supposedly posted their lines all over the set as backup.

Peter would kill to have a part like that someday. But despite what Natalie thought, he wouldn't use a friend to get it.

Yeah, right, he told himself. *That's exactly what you did during the fall. You were using a friend to help you get ahead as an actor. It's just that, although you didn't know it, you were using a friend who didn't have any more showbiz connections than you do.*

It made complete sense that Natalie thought he'd been trying to show off his acting chops to her tonight, hoping she'd say something to her dad. Man, she'd been furious. She hadn't said much, but she hadn't had to. It was all over her face.

He should have stuck with the avoidance plan. True, he wouldn't have been able to avoid her during cheerleading practice. But he could have tried to blend, lay low.

Now everything was even more messed up. Natalie hated him even more than she had before.

Peter hadn't thought that was even possible.

chapter

EIGHT

Miles held a cheerleading sweater up in front of him at cheerleading practice the next day. "Too small," he said.

Of course it's too small, Natalie thought. The guys were being all Goldilocks today. Except they never got to the *and-this-cheerleading-outfit-is-just-right* stage. Nope, nothing fit. Nothing was good enough. She definitely wasn't a good enough coach to get them motivated.

Not that Joanna was, either. In fact, Joanna wasn't even there. She hadn't asked Natalie if it was okay to skip. She hadn't even told Natalie she was skipping. Nope, she'd just skipped. What was wrong with her this weekend?

Miles tossed the cheerleading sweater back in the pile. Ellie had supplied a bunch of gear guys had worn for the annual powder-puff game at her high school.

Peter picked up another sweater and looked over at Miles. "Looks like this one will fit you."

"It might fit right now," Miles admitted. "But I don't have my stuffing on. I doubt any of them will fit once I'm stuffed," he added, sounding happy at the thought.

Oh, great. Were the guys planning to stuff? *Not classy. Not cute. Not gonna happen*, she thought.

"You don't have anything to put your stuffing *in*," David told him. He lowered his voice, but not low enough. Natalie still heard him say, "Because we didn't fulfill our mission the other night. We have no bras."

Peter and a couple other guys jerked their heads toward Natalie. The picture of Peter holding her bra flashed through her brain. Yuck.

"You don't have them, and you're not going to need them," Natalie informed them.

"I bet this one will probably fit me okay," Peter said. He pulled off his sweatshirt, and yanked on the cheerleading sweater Miles had rejected. Then he turned in a circle, arms thrown out. "It's fine. See?"

"Peter's a little too eager to get into girls' clothes, don't you think?" Ben joked. "I guess I can see why. He's verrry pretty."

Guys are such idiots. All of them, Natalie thought. "Can I have a little maturity out of you?" she demanded.

"Yeah, you guys. We're trying to get that Spirit Award, remember?" Peter asked. "We can't let the Talamini guys be better cheerleaders than we are."

I asked for a little maturity, Natalie thought. *Not a little sarcasm*. She checked the clock. It had been almost half an hour and they hadn't even started working on a routine. How long did it really take to grab a cheerleading outfit? For these guys—guys who didn't want to be here—a long, long time.

"Look. Either find yourself an outfit, or I'll find one for you," she snapped. "I want you all dressed in three minutes. Three!"

A couple guys made the going-to-the-principal sound. "Ooooooh."

Justin raised his hand. Natalie was almost positive she didn't want to know what he was going to say. "Yes?" she said, anyway.

"I would love to get dressed," Justin told her. "But I don't have the proper underwear."

"No bras! No stuffing!" Natalie barked.

"That's not what I was talking about," Justin said politely, although Natalie noticed his lips were twitching, like he was trying hard not to laugh. "I mean, I'm wearing boxers. Cheerleaders don't wear boxers under their skirts. They wear those things . . . slappies."

"Spankies," Peter corrected. All the guys, and Natalie, looked at him. "I've seen some cheerleader movies," Peter explained.

The guys laughed. *Thanks, Peter*, Natalie thought, *for adding to the comedy show*. As if things weren't out of control enough already.

"Whatever they're called, I'm not doing cartwheels without them," Justin said.

"We have to do cartwheels?" Connor complained.

"Haven't you seen some of the moves guy cheerleaders do?" Peter asked, pulling a short, pleated skirt over his jeans. "It's just as much of a sport as football. You need coordination. Strength."

That's almost exactly what I said yesterday, Natalie thought. Was he imitating her?

He was! He had to be.

The guys thought so, too. Look at all them laughing. This was never going to work. Never!

Natalie wasn't going to just stand here and take their abuse. She needed some air. She rushed out the front door and slammed it behind her as hard as she could.

▲ ▲ ▲

What went on down there at practice? Joanna wondered. From the bedroom window, she'd seen Natalie storm out, and she'd heard the door slam all the way upstairs. Now Peter was heading over toward football practice, head down, hands jammed in his pockets.

I should have been there, she thought, feeling a spurt of guilt. It looked like Natalie had needed her. But it wasn't like Joanna had any control over the guys, either. And she'd really wanted to write a letter to her mom.

She looked down at her notebook, reading what she had so far:

Dear Mom,

It's really beautiful here at the lodge. And it's great to be with all my friends. We had a dance last night, and I'm helping coach the boys' cheerleading squad. The guys are cheering for the girls who are playing a powder-puff football game. If they're good, we might win a Spirit trophy, which would be cool.

Well, it's cheerful, Joanna thought. She'd been going for cheerful. The book she'd found last night had a whole chapter on how a positive attitude was essential for healing. Which is why she wanted her letter to be super cheerful.

And everything she'd written was true. It *was* beautiful here. There *had* been a dance. She was helping coach the guys. Sort of. At least she had at the first practice. Kind of.

Didn't matter. It's not like her mom would ever know. Joanna began to read again:

How are you feeling? Have you been obeying my Post-its? =) I know I left a lot of them, but there's a lot of important stuff you need to remember. Like keeping your dressing dry. I wish you'd been able to have laparoscopic surgery. You'd heal so much faster, but sometimes traditional surgery is more appropriate. I'm sure Dr. Templeton was right.

So, just remember to keep the dressing dry, so you don't get an infection. Even if you're careful, you might get one, anyway. You'll know because the incision site will be red and puffy, and you'll get a fever, and—

Joanna crumbled the letter into a ball and threw it on the floor. What had she been thinking? That part was not cheerful at all. It was scary. And besides, even if she started over and wrote a perfectly happy letter, it wouldn't get to her mother before Joanna got home, anyway.

If her mom and dad were still together, he'd be home with her right now. And her father would be able to keep her mom smiling. He was good at that.

Well, he'd *been* good at it. Joanna realized that her mind had gone to memories long in the past. It had probably been more than two years since her mother had managed to smile with Joanna's dad in the same room.

I shouldn't be here, Joanna thought. *Mom shouldn't be alone. How can she keep a positive attitude sitting there all by herself?*

Yeah, friends would stop by. But that wasn't the same. Her mother needed Joanna this weekend. Her camp friends didn't.

▲ ▲ ▲

Avery veered across the field, eyes locked on the spiraling football flying toward her. *Yes, yes, yes.* She reached up, and the ball smacked into her hands. She tightened her grip on it, clutched it tight to her chest, and kept on running.

Footsteps pounded behind her. Getting closer. A lot closer. *Bam!* Avery felt someone's shoulder smack into her side. She staggered a few steps, but then regained her speed. *That hit was off the mark,* she thought. *Too high.*

Avery grinned. Everyone couldn't be as talented as she was—couldn't and weren't. She surveyed the field. A zig there, a zag here, and touchdown! She spiked the ball, and then did her TD dance. She thought it was the TD dance Beyonce would do. Sharp. Sexy. Avery.

"And that's practice!" Jenna called.

Sarah slapped Avery on the back. "Who knew?" She shook her head. "I—you—who knew?"

Avery laughed, but her laughter trailed off when she spotted Peter on the sidelines. He looked . . . pathetic. Like a sad little boy. *I guess I better go see what's wrong,* she thought. *Big sigh.* But, to be fair, Peter mostly had been doing fine on his own at the reunion.

She walked over to her twin. "How's it going?"

"Fine. Good," he answered.

"Liar."

"Horrible," Peter admitted as they started down one of the winding trails that ran around the lodge.

"I suppose you should tell me," Avery told him. "Go on, talk," she added when he hesitated.

"Natalie hates me," Peter said.

"Well . . . that's not exactly a news flash, right? You knew that before we left home," Avery answered. "I'm guessing the avoidance plan isn't working out so well."

"It's working okay with Sarah," Peter told her. "But since I got forced onto the cheerleading squad—"

"Avoiding Natalie is impossible," Avery finished for him. She hadn't even thought about that. She hadn't been thinking much about Peter. She'd been having too much fun playing football hero.

"Whatever's harder than impossible, that's what it is," Peter agreed. He reached out and knocked the thin line of snow off the branch of the nearest pine tree.

"There's still my plan," Avery said. "Apologizing."

"No," Peter replied. "Apologizing means having to talk about the reason she hates me. That could make her hate me even more."

"Possible, I guess," Avery admitted. "But what other choice do you have?"

"I basically decided I was going to be extra, extra nice to her," Peter said. "But it's not working. Partly because Ben asked me to do my Bruce Campbell in *Evil Dead* 2 impression when I was talking to her."

Avery groaned. "And she thought you were trying to get to her dad through her."

"Yep. The thing is, the talking part was going okay, until that," Peter said. "More than okay, actually."

Avery stopped and stared at him.

"What?" Peter finally asked.

"You like her. You like Natalie!" Avery accused.

"I just wanted to make it up to her, for what I did back when I was an extra with Brynn and Sarah," Peter protested.

"And how much time have you spent trying to be extra, extra nice to Sarah, who, if you remember, is the girl you actually pretended to like?" Avery asked.

"I did like Sarah. I just didn't *like her*—like her," Peter explained.

"The way you *like*-like Natalie," Avery said. Her brother looked confused. No wonder relationships with guys were so impossible. Boys were clueless. Peter genuinely didn't know how he felt about Nat, while Avery had figured it out in a couple minutes.

"Natalie. I was having a pretty good time with her," Peter answered. "And you should see her with the cheerleading guys. She's in our faces. She doesn't let anyone get away with anything."

"That's unusual for you. You can usually charm everyone you meet," Avery said.

"Like you can't," Peter shot back.

Avery did a hair flip. "I use my powers for good. Mostly," she answered.

Peter snorted. "I've been trying with Natalie. Like today at practice, I tried to back her up. I tried to help her get the guys motivated. But she looked just as furious at me as she did with the rest of them."

"You have some major damage control to do," Avery said. "Especially because you like her."

Peter's brow furrowed. "I'm heading back," he told her.

He's still trying to figure out if he really does like her, Avery thought. *Pitiful*.

As she continued to stroll down the path, a few thick flakes of snow began to fall. So pretty. They started to come faster, much faster. Snow was clinging to her eyelashes and sticking to the shoulders of her jacket.

Avery stopped and tilted her head back. "No," she ordered the gray sky. "I'm not having it. Tomorrow's game will not be snowed out, do you understand? I'm going to win the game for Walla Walla!"

chapter NINE

"It's really coming down," Justin commented.

"Ay-yup," Ben agreed.

"Ay-yup," David agreed.

And they just kept going, trading *ay-yups*.

"It's this thing from this local radio show they both listen to," Miles explained to Peter, seeing his raised eyebrow. "Correction. It's this *stupid* thing from this local radio show they both listen to. The talk jocks pretend to be these two old men who sit around all day agreeing with each other."

"Ay-yup," David agreed.

"Ay-yup," Ben agreed.

"It can go on for hours," Miles added. Ben and David gave the expected response.

Usually Peter would jump in, try to imitate the weird accent they had going. It was definitely some kind of New England dialect. Maine? But tonight he was distracted. He kept thinking about the conversation he'd had with Avery this afternoon. Could his sister be right? Could he like Natalie? *Like*-like?

He shot a look at Nat, who was eating with her girls at the next table. She was totally beautiful, yeah. But she hated him. You weren't supposed to like someone who hated you. It made no sense.

"PETER, PLEASE PASS THE KETCHUP," Connor said very loudly. Like he'd already asked at least three times.

"Sorry," Peter muttered, sliding the ketchup across the table.

"I think we're definitely going to be able to go sledding tomorrow," Connor said.

Peter followed Connor's gaze, watching the falling snow through the big dining room windows. "There's this killer hill in back of the lodge. We'll add some moguls to it. All we have to do is pack down the snow really hard to make them. It will be *monster*."

Peter started to turn his attention from the snow back to Connor, but his eyes snagged on something. Natalie. *Still beautiful*, he thought. *Still hates you*, he added.

But at the dance, for a couple minutes, she'd gotten over it. He was sure she had. She'd stopped hating him. When they were dancing together, it really felt like she'd stopped hating. She'd even laughed at something he said.

Then he'd blown it acting out that movie scene.

"PETER, HOW MANY INCHES YOU THINK WE'LL GET IF IT KEEPS UP LIKE THIS UNTIL MORNING?" Connor asked very loudly, like he'd already said the same thing a few times.

"What's so interesting over there?" David asked. He leaned back so he could see what Peter had been staring at. Then he stared at Peter. "Natalie," he announced to the table. "Peter was staring at Natalie."

"Just a heads up? She hates you," Justin said.

"Ay-yup," Connor chimed in.

"Ay-yup," David agreed. "But you don't hate her, do you?" he asked Peter. "Are you one of those guys who only likes girls who will never like them? That's a type of mental illness," he joked.

"That's why you were all rah-rah at practice," Connor accused.

"I wasn't all anything," Peter protested.

"You were like a Natalie parrot," Ben told him. "Now, boys, let's do this for Walla Walla," he said in a high voice that sounded nothing like Nat, and absolutely nothing like Peter.

"You do like her, don't you?" Miles asked.

"No," Peter answered. "Like David said, that would be a kind of mental illness. I'm not mentally ill."

"Yeah, you are," Miles said, studying him.

Ben and David gave a few rounds of *ay-yups*, only stopping when they were both laughing so hard they seemed mentally ill themselves.

"Come on. Like you two have never liked somebody who doesn't like you," Connor said. "I have. I admit it. Once, I actually wrote a poem. Seriously. I was that pathetic."

"I can top that," Justin said. "My cousin went to this school that had a bear as a mascot. We smuggled out the mascot costume—just long enough for me to go to this girl's house with some red and pink balloons."

"Wait. What does that have to do with a bear?" Ben asked.

Justin got very busy with his hamburger.

"You brought it up. You have to tell us," Ben said.

"I also carried a sign." He took another huge bite of burger. "It said, 'I'm Your Teddy Bear.'"

"How much blue punch did you drink before you came up with that plan?" Miles asked.

"I was completely artificial-color and other bad chemical free," Justin admitted.

"You might have to sleep in the hall," David told him. "I'm not sure I can be your bunkmate after hearing that story."

Peter glanced over at Natalie. How would she react to a teddy bear costume? Sarah caught him staring at Nat and glared at him. He jerked his eyes away. "Did the girl like it?" he asked Ben.

"Let's just say I had to pay to have the costume dry-cleaned," Ben said. "Some items were thrown. Messy ones. That's the kind of thing that happens when you try to make nice with girls who hate you."

Natalie probably wouldn't like the teddy bear any better than the girl Justin liked had, Peter decided. But he was suddenly hit with an idea for something she might like. Might really like.

Something that would convince her he was done trying to use her—or anyone he thought was her—to get ahead in his acting career. Something that might get her to look at him the way she had when they were dancing. Like he was just a guy, not a monster.

▲ ▲ ▲

"Nat, you're going to have to come up with a cheer just for Avery," Sarah said. "She's turned out to be a pro. Major-league all the way."

"Pshaw." Avery flipped one hand dismissively, then she gave a grin. "Well, my own cheer might be kind of nice. It could be for when I tackle someone. I've discovered I have a talent for tackling. Also eluding being tackled. Catching. Throwing. Kicking. Touchdowning."

"Modesty," Priya teased, tossing a little piece of hamburger bun at Avery.

"And that," Avery agreed, throwing the bit of bun back.

"I'll be lucky if I can get the guys in their uniforms and on the field tomorrow," Natalie admitted.

"Really? It's that bad?" Brynn asked Joanna. "Or is Nat exaggerating?"

Like Joanna would know, Natalie thought. *She's invisible at practices, when she bothers to show.*

Joanna gave a noncommittal shrug.

"I'm not exaggerating. I know I kept saying I could lead the cheerleaders to vic-tor-y, but prepare yourselves. If the Talamini guys completely suck, they'll still be hugely better than our guys. There's no way we're going to be able to bring home the Spirit trophy."

"It's not like you to give up," Jenna commented.

"I know." Natalie let her head fall into her hands for

109

a moment, then looked up at her friends. "And I know I should be saying I'm going to whip them into shape, but I really don't know how. I think it's doomed."

"Cookies," Sarah suggested. "Guys will usually perform for cookies."

"If you put M&Ms in them Jordan would do anything. He lives for his junk food when he's away from home," Priya commented.

"I bet you could talk the cooks into letting us bake a batch," Brynn suggested.

"I'm not rewarding them for bad behavior," Natalie answered. "Not even if you make a dozen double-chocolate-chip and M&M cookies just for me."

"This is serious," Jenna joked. "Chocolate is not motivating Natalie."

"Forget about the guys—at least for now," Natalie said. "How's the team doing—other than the fabulous Avery? Think we have a shot at beating Talamini?" Natalie asked.

"Oh, yeah," Sarah answered. "We are so going to bring it."

"And Walla Walla's getting the Sports trophy back," Jenna added.

They both sounded super-confident. *At least Walla Walla will get one trophy this year*, Natalie thought. That won't be so bad.

"It's starting to snow pretty hard," Joanna said. "Do you think we'll even be able to have the game? Maybe we'll be sent home early."

"You almost sound happy about the idea," Natalie accused.

"No!" Joanna protested. "It was just, you know, a question."

"Well, don't worry, Jo. No matter how much it snows, you'll be warm and dry." Jenna winked at her, smiling. "You look like a marshmallow you have so many layers on."

"It's true!" Priya agreed. "A round, soft, yummy marshmallow."

Joanna jumped up so fast, the legs of her chair screeched against the planks of the wood floor. Without even looking back, she headed for the stairs that led to her room.

Jenna held both hands up. "I was just kidding. You guys know that, right? I'm Jenna, the kidder."

"I didn't mean anything bad. I said 'yummy.' Yummy is good." Priya glanced around the table, getting nods of support.

"Let's go apologize, anyway," Jenna said to Priya.

"Wait," Natalie told them. "Let me go talk to her. She's been acting weird this whole weekend. Not just at cheerleading practices, either. I'm going to ask her what's going on."

"Finish eating first," Chelsea suggested.

"Not hungry," Natalie answered. She wasn't. She felt too bad to eat. Not just about the stupid, stupid, selfish guys on her so-called squad. Not just because Joanna was being all freaky. It was also because of Peter. She shot a glance at him. He was laughing with the boys, having a great time. Like he hadn't slimed her last night, trying to audition for her dad by performing for her.

She stood up, making sure to slide her chair back gently. That screeching sound Joanna had made with hers had made Natalie's teeth ache. Then she walked across the dining room, head up, smiling, in case anyone—like Peter—was watching. She slowly climbed up the main stairs. She was in no hurry to have this conversation with Joanna. But it had to be done.

Natalie softly opened the door to the bedroom. Joanna sat on her bed, with her comforter wrapped tightly around her shoulders.

"We have to talk," Natalie said.

Joanna reluctantly shut the book she held in her lap. "I shouldn't have run out of dinner. I know everyone was just joking. I don't know what's wrong with me."

"I don't, either." Natalie sat down on the bed across from Joanna's. "You haven't been *you* for the whole reunion."

"I'm really sorry," Joanna answered. "I didn't help at all during cheerleading practice. I completely let you down."

"Yeah, you did," Natalie told her. "But that's not what I'm talking about. Not really."

"But I—"

Natalie didn't let Joanna continue. She had something important to say to her friend. "You've been keeping to yourself so much. It's like you don't want to hang out with the rest of us—even though we haven't seen one another for months, and we won't see one another again until summer. You didn't dance at all the other night. You just hid on the sidelines and read."

Natalie took Joanna's book from her. "What are you reading that's so fascinating, anyway?"

Natalie checked the book's cover, then frowned. "You're reading a book on home remedies?"

"I keep thinking about my mom," Joanna admitted.

"But after she had her surgery, you posted that it went really well," Natalie said. "Did something happen? Why didn't you say something?"

"Nothing happened It's only that— " Joanna twisted the comforter in her hands. "You know my parents split . . ."

Natalie nodded. "Back before Christmas."

"Yeah," Joanna answered. "And that means, without me, my mom's all alone. I keep thinking I should be there. The operation went great, but the doctor gave my mom this whole list of things to do and watch out for. She's not supposed to lift anything heavy. She's not supposed to skip any doses of her medicine. She's supposed to keep checking the incision site to make sure it's not infected."

Natalie leaned forward. "You don't think your mom will be doing all that?"

"I don't know," Joanna admitted. "Usually when she gets sick or something my dad goes into super-caretaker mode. This is the first time he hasn't been there for her. I really wanted to stay home, but she practically pushed me out the door."

"She wanted you to have fun," Natalie said. "And you'll be home really soon. It's already Sunday night. In less than twenty-four hours, we'll all be heading home." She reached out and covered Joanna's hands with one of hers. "Can you try to have a good time until then?"

"I guess," Joanna answered.

"You know your mom's going to ask if you did. You're going to need some good stuff to report. So why don't you come back downstairs," Natalie coaxed.

"Okay." Joanna shrugged off her comforter and stood up. "I wish I could just talk to her for a minute. I asked my dad to check in on her. I want to make sure he did."

"Why haven't you called?" Natalie asked.

"No cells allowed. You know the rule," Joanna answered.

"Are you forgetting who's in charge of this place? Dr. Steve is not going to say no if you want to talk to your mom when she's recovering from surgery." Natalie headed for the door. "Come on. Let's go find him."

Joanna smiled. A real smile. She pulled off her top sweatshirt. It looked like she had about three more layers on. "It doesn't feel as cold to me anymore."

"Hand it over," Natalie said. "I'm freezing!"

chapter
TEN

Sloan couldn't sleep. She flipped over her pillow. It was nice and cool, but it didn't help. She felt a tiny lump—well, more of a wrinkle—under one thigh, and she smoothed the sheets out. Didn't help. She turned over onto her right side. Didn't help. Turned onto her left side. Didn't help. Flipped onto her stomach. Didn't help. Went back to her usual sleeping position—on her back with one hand curled up under her chin. Didn't work.

The problem wasn't with how she was lying on the bed. It had nothing to do with a warm pillow or bunched up sheets. No, the problem was the quiet. It was just too quiet in her room. Sloan could hear the other girls breathing, and somebody—she thought it was Jenna—had a cute, snuffly little snore going. But on top of all those little sounds—silence.

The silence made Sloan think of snow. Layer after layer of soft snow coating everything. Muffling everything. *It's not as if not snow creates a sound*, she told herself. *Snow and not-snow sound the same.*

But it was still snowing. Sloan could feel it. And

that's what was keeping her awake. She threw off the covers and hurried over to the window. She peered out into the darkness. The darkness and the whiteness. The snow hadn't stopped. Actually, it was coming down harder than it had before.

At least we didn't get evacuated early, Sloan told herself. *The reunion didn't get shut down.* And Sloan was there, seeing all her friends. Snow now didn't matter that much. She wasn't worried about getting home safely. If her flight was delayed, she'd be at Dr. Steve's.

But she'd seen how hard her friends had been working on their football skills. The game would be canceled if it kept up like this. Which it would. Of course it would. Her aunt Willow really was a genius about predicting the weather, especially with the help of the birds and bears and all. It's like Willow had a direct line to Mother Nature.

Mother Nature. That gave Sloan an idea. She walked over to Jenna's bed and gave her friend a gentle shake. Jenna woke up in mid-snuffly snore.

"What? Was I snoring? People always say I snore, but I don't," Jenna said.

"No. Or, actually, yes. You were snoring, but it wasn't very loud and that's not why I woke you up," Sloan answered.

"So why?" Jenna asked, sitting up.

"I want to tell everyone at once. Help me wake people up—everybody next door. Maybe all the girls on the football team? No," Sloan answered her own question. "This has to be a secret mission. Secret and stealthy. If we get too many people, both those things will be impossible."

"I'm still sort of half-asleep," Jenna said. "Either that, or you're not making sense."

"I'm probably not," Sloan admitted. "Just go get Sarah, Brynn, Avery, Priya, and Chelsea—without waking up Ellie or any other counselor types. Bring them over here, and I'll explain everything."

Jenna blinked a few times, then swung her legs off the bed and stood up. "Okay. I don't know why, but okay."

Sloan tiptoed over to Natalie's bed. She leaned down until her lips were almost against Nat's ear. "Wake up," she whispered. Natalie batted at her face, then rolled onto her side. Sloan tried again, a little louder. "Nat, wake up!"

"What's going on?" Joanna asked. She leaned over and reached for the light switch.

"Leave it off," Sloan ordered. "And shhhh!"

Natalie jerked awake, almost knocking Sloan off the bed. "What's wrong?"

"Shhh!" Sloan told her. "And nothing. Nothing's wrong. I just have an idea, but I need help with it."

"And the help couldn't come—I don't know—in the morning?" Natalie asked.

Sloan started to answer, but was interrupted by Jenna creeping back into the room, followed by Brynn, Avery, Sarah, Priya, and Chelsea. Both Avery's and Chelsea's faces were a weird pale blue. It took Sloan a few seconds to realize they must have shared some kind of face mask.

"If I'm going to perform tomorrow, I need my

sleep," Avery complained.

"There won't be a game to perform in if it doesn't stop snowing." Sloan fished her flashlight out from under her bed and shone it out the window. They all stared at the whiteness.

"I don't think staring at it is going to change anything," Chelsea muttered.

"But it might! Or it sort of might. It's not just staring. It's more like staring and thinking and *intending*. That's why I need you all," Sloan said.

"Can I be the first to say 'huh'?" Jenna asked. She put her hands in the pockets of her flannel pajama bottoms.

"Look, just trust me. Please," Sloan told them. "Trust me, and follow me, and I'll explain. Oh, and you'll need boots and coats." She grabbed her coat out of the closet.

"You didn't tell us that," Chelsea complained.

"She didn't tell me to tell you that!" Jenna answered.

"Shhh!" Sloan warned. She grabbed her coat out of the closet. "Get ready and meet me downstairs by the front door." She didn't want to tell them her idea until they were outside. They might all go back to bed without trying her plan if she did.

About six minutes later, they were all gathered by the door. "Follow me," Sloan told them. She opened the door. She had to hold the doorknob tightly so the wind didn't rip the door out of her hand. The sound of it banging against the front of the lodge would wake at least one person up.

Sloan held the door until all her friends had trooped outside. Then she carefully shut it, making sure to leave it unlocked. She signaled the other girls to follow her and led the way down the nearest trail until they came to a small clearing. Trees shielded them on all sides.

"Okay, start talking," Jenna said.

"We're going to do a ceremony to stop the snow and bring fair weather for tomorrow's game," Sloan announced.

"You're kidding!" Avery burst out. She looked at Sloan for a long moment. Sloan looked back. "You aren't kidding," Avery concluded. "But you should be. You should absolutely be kidding."

"The last time you got us involved with all your woo-woo stuff it *started* a snowstorm, remember?" Chelsea asked.

"Well, no amethysts this time," Sloan said. "I went to a workshop with my parents a few months ago," Sloan began to explain. "It was about how people's wishes could have an effect on the weather. The guy giving the talk used Princeton as an example. They have these year-end ceremonies that involve a whole bunch of people being outside, so many that it would be almost impossible to move the events inside. And the weather is almost always good. It's good more than it statistically should be." Sloan took a gulp of cold air, and kept on talking. "I think we should do a ceremony, letting Mother Nature know what our wishes are for tomorrow's weather."

"Like a rain dance that Native Americans used to do?" Sarah asked.

"Kind of. Except we don't want rain. Or snow. We

want no snow. Or rain," Sloan said. "And the ceremony is just a way for us to focus our intentions. The power of people's thoughts is much more powerful than anyone knows."

"I'm suddenly remembering that you're from Sedona," Avery said. "Capital of woo-woo."

"That's right—because of all the natural power vortexes—places where the earth's lines of cosmic power intersect and create this awesome force field," Sloan corrected her. "That's been proven. And that's why a lot of people visit when they are on a spiritual journey."

Avery threw out her arms in a see-what-I'm-dealing-with-here gesture of frustration.

Sarah spoke up. "I think we should try it. Sloan's right. If it keeps snowing like this, our game's going to be canceled. What can it hurt to try?"

"I'm in," Jenna said.

"Me too," Joanna volunteered.

"I'm already out here, freezing my knees," Chelsea added. "Let's do it."

Sloan hesitated. "You don't know what we're supposed to be doing, do you?" Natalie asked.

"Like I said, a ceremony is just a way to focus our energy. It doesn't matter exactly what we do, we just have to do something." Sloan felt like she was losing them. She clapped her hands, trying to imitate Jenna and Sarah when they were coaching. "Everybody in a circle, arms width apart."

Her coach voice worked. The girls formed a circle in the center of the clearing. They stretched out their arms to make sure they were standing the correct distance apart.

Sloan joined the circle, her mind whirling. What next? "Snow angels!" she exclaimed. "Everybody lie down and make a snow angel. The wings should just be touching when you're done."

Sloan dropped to the ground. She smiled as everyone else did, too. They all swept their arms and legs out and back until they had created a circle of angles. "Now stand up," Sloan instructed. "Carefully. Don't put footprints on the angels."

She moved into the center of the angel circle. "Everybody in!" she called. "Now look up, right up into the falling snow, and thank Mother Nature for it. Just however you want to do it. However you feel like it."

Sloan threw her arms up and tilted her head back, letting the snow hit her full in the face. "Thank you for this wonderful, beautiful stuff."

"Thanks for giving us snow for snowballs," Jenna chimed in.

When everyone had given thanks, Sloan lowered her arms. "Now we all have to send out the same wish. A wish for the snow to stop long enough for us to have our game," she said. "Close your eyes, and wish, wish, wish."

Sloan followed her own instructions. And as she wished, she was sure she could feel her friends' wishes flying around her, joining her wish, and soaring out into the universe.

"I think we've done all we can," she finally said. In silence, they returned to the lodge. Tomorrow they'd know if what they'd done was enough.

Avery climbed out of bed the next morning and went immediately to the window. The snow had stopped, but outside, the whole world was white. Clumps of snow clung to all the tree branches. Avery couldn't even tell where the driveway was. Not a speck of it was showing through the thick whiteness.

"How does it look, Ave?" Brynn asked.

"It looks like we were doing a ceremony *for* snow, not to prevent it," Avery told her.

"I warned her, didn't I? I said that we'd started a snowstorm the last time and we did it again!" Chelsea exclaimed.

"I don't know why I was expecting anything different. I'm not that into Sloan's woo-woo, Mother Nature–loving, Sedona stuff," Avery commented.

"It was fun, though," Sarah said, sitting up.

"Yeah. Maybe the last fun we're going to have. I don't know if I'm going to be able to demonstrate my newfound greatness on the field today. Not with all that white gunk."

"I guess if we have to forfeit, Talamini gets to keep both trophies for another year," Chelsea commented.

"It's not the same as winning them," Sarah answered.

"It's still not good, though," Chelsea said.

"Not even remotely good," Avery agreed.

Brynn pulled a pair of jeans out of the dresser. "Let's get dressed and get down to breakfast. I'm sure Dr. Steve will give us the news first thing."

Twenty minutes later, Avery led her roomies

downstairs and into the dining room. Natalie, Sloan, Jenna, and Joanna were already at their table. *Joanna hasn't slipped back into her funk,* Avery thought, noting the smile on her friend's face. She didn't know what kind of chewing out or pepping up Natalie had administered to Joanna the night before, but it was still in effect.

"Any word on whether the game can go on or not?" Avery asked as she sat down.

"Not yet," Jenna answered.

"We have to be able to play," Sarah said. "We've got such an amazing team. And all of you worked like Amazon women."

"Let's wait to see what Dr. Steve says before we get all upset," Priya suggested.

Brynn gave a loud sniff. "It smells like we're having chocolate-chip pancakes," she said. "Which—yum. But could the kitchen crew be feeling sorry for us? Do they know something we don't know?"

"There's Dr. Steve!" Avery exclaimed. He was striding toward the front of the room, and he had his concerned look on his face.

"Good morning, gang!" Dr. Steve called.

Everyone said good morning back, but the greeting wasn't nearly as loud as Walla Walla campers usually made it.

Jenna cupped her hands to her mouth and yelled, "Does the game go on, Dr. Steve?"

"I've just been on the phone with Mr. Billingham, the head of Camp Talamini," he answered. "Right now, the Talamini campers can't get over here. The roads are impassable, even with chains."

Now the Walla Walla campers showed exactly how much noise they could make. Groans and moans were coming from every direction. Avery added in her own wail of frustration.

Dr. Steve held both arms in the air and made patting motions with his hands. "Hang on, hang on!" he told the group. "I didn't finish. The snowplows will be out soon. We're going to have to push the game from this morning to early afternoon, when the roads will be clear. But the annual powder-puff battle between Talamini and Walla Walla *will* happen!"

Avery thought the sad sounds had been loud. The cheers almost blew off the roof.

"I think we deserve some of the credit," Sloan told the group. She started slapping high fives, leaning across the table so she didn't miss anyone.

Avery grinned at her. "I swear, I now love Sedona and all its woo-woo-osity." She threw back her head. "Talamini, get ready for the new, improved, football-playing Avery!"

▲ ▲ ▲

Joanna was laughing so hard it was almost impossible to keep her grip on the edges of the sled as it whooshed down the snow-covered hill behind the lodge. "Big bump coming up on our left!" Natalie shouted from her seat behind Joanna.

Joanna leaned as far left as she could without falling off. "I wasn't telling you so you could—" Natalie's words turned into a scream as they hit the bump and went airborne.

"There isn't a big, big bump coming up on the right," Natalie yelled in Joanna's ear. Joanna grinned as she leaned hard to the right, steering the sled right to the mogul.

"Whee!" she cried as they went airborne again. Joanna loved that feeling, where her stomach jumped up into her chest, then plunged back down. "Let's get back up to the top and do it again!" she exclaimed when the sled slid to a stop at the bottom of the hill.

"Give me a second." Natalie adjusted the pom-pom on the top of her stocking cap. She looked like a cute little elf, especially with her cheeks all pink from the ride down.

"Ready?" Joanna asked her.

Natalie laughed. "Am I really the one who told you to make sure and have fun?"

"Yep, that was you!" And Joanna *was* having fun. Her mom was doing great. Her dad had come through. He'd checked up on her mother, just the way he'd said he would. There'd been pretty much the perfect amount of snow—enough for awesome sledding, not too much to force the camps to cancel the football game.

"Well, let's get back up there, then. But I'm steering this time." Natalie grabbed the sled's rope and started hauling it up the hill.

"Nat, Joanna! We need you!" Brynn shouted before they were even halfway to the top.

As soon as Joanna and Natalie flew down the hill again, they hurried over to Brynn. She had most of the football team gathered around. "I want to make a huge snow kitty over by the bleachers on our side of the field. I want Talamini to know we mean business the second they arrive."

"And nothing says 'fear us' like a giant kitty made out of snow," Jenna joked.

"As soon as I make my first tackle, they're going to be afraid," Avery promised.

"The boys should be helping us make the fear cat," Chelsea said. "They could show a little spirit that way, since they aren't bothering to practice their cheerleading."

"Even if they didn't want to do that, they're missing all the snow fun," Brynn said. "Those guys love tubing down the hill. That's practically all they did the last winter reunion we had at Lakeview."

"That and snow wars," Jenna agreed. She reached into her coat pocket, pulled out a snowball, and threw it at Brynn.

Brynn squealed, then dropped to the ground and started throwing handfuls of snow back at Jenna.

"Loose snow isn't the way to do it," Joanna told her. "You can't get any real velocity with—" Before she finished her sentence, Brynn had her on the ground.

"Nice tackle!" Avery called.

Brynn stuffed a handful of snow down Joanna's back. It turned her spine to ice. Joanna let out a sound that was half-shriek and half-laugh. She scooped up a fistful of snow and smushed it into Brynn's face. "Maybe you're right," Joanna told her. "Maybe loose snow is good."

"She got you, Brynn," Natalie said.

A look flashed between Brynn and Joanna. They both grinned. Then they each made a snowball and lobbed them at Natalie at the same time.

Natalie pulled off her hat and wiped the snow off the front of her coat. "Did I really, really, *really* tell you to try and have more fun?" she asked Joanna, shaking her head and smiling. "What was I thinking?"

chapter ELEVEN

"This is going to be so much cooler than any prank you guys ever pulled," Peter promised Ben, David, Justin, Connor, and Miles. "It's going to be fun, too. I swear." They were gathered in the second floor hallway. The sound of everybody else playing in the snow outside was audible even through the closed windows.

"First, you don't know the complete history of our pranks," David said. "And second, are you saying what you have planned is going to be more fun than sledding, and tubing, and snow forts, and snowball war? Because that's what we could be doing right this second."

"Yes," Peter answered quickly. He could tell David was saying what all the other guys were feeling. He didn't need a mutiny. He had to keep control of the group. "Look. Think about the practices we had. Think about Natalie at those practices. She deserves this," he told them.

He looked from guy to guy. "Are you in? Are we going to give Natalie what she needs?"

Connor answered first. "Yeah."

A couple guys hesitated, but Peter ended up with a yes from everyone. He'd had to start giving away his DVDs to do it, though, and the ones he'd brought with him were his favorites.

Now comes the hard part of the plan, he thought. *Am I going to be able to pull this off?*

▲ ▲ ▲

"It was so great to talk to my mom," Joanna told Natalie after lunch, as they headed toward the football field for the big game. "She's been following all the doctor's instructions, and a couple of her friends have come by. I know I told you that already. But it was just so great hearing her voice! I would have known if she was feeling bad. I know her fake 'I'm-great' voice. And that was not the voice she was using last night." She gave a little hop.

"Never underestimate Dr. Steve and his willingness to bend a rule if there's a good reason," Natalie answered.

"I told you my dad had checked to see if she needed anything, right?" Joanna asked.

Natalie smiled. "I think you mentioned that a couple times last night, and maybe three times before breakfast. Then at breakfast."

"It's just that that's a big thing," Joanna said, her eyes sparkling. Maybe they'll actually end up friends someday. They keep telling me they already are, but I know it's not true. Come on. I'm not five. I haven't believed in Santa Claus or the tooth fairy in a couple years."

"Wait up, you guys!"

Natalie looked over her shoulder and saw Sarah rushing toward them, snow flying up around her with every step.

"Hey, it's one of the captains that's going to bring glory and honor to Walla Walla!" Joanna called.

"Any update on the cheerleaders?" Sarah asked.

"We had a brief sighting of them in the hall outside their bedrooms before lunch, but they scurried away like scared bunnies when they saw us. And I'm sure you saw how they all bolted down their food and disappeared again," Natalie answered. "We decided it was pointless to track them down. They don't want to practice, I can't make them. Even if I'm right in their faces, yelling."

"Maybe it'll be just as well if they don't show. Nothing worse than a halfhearted cheerleader," Joanna agreed.

"Really? I think not having any cheerleaders would be horrible. Like Walla Walla has no camp spirit at all," Natalie replied. "Even though the guys refused to take practice seriously, I'm sure they're still going to at least show up. I'm just afraid the Talamini cheerleaders will be a million times better."

"Nat, have you considered—" Sarah hesitated. "Do you think maybe Peter could be behind the whole disappearing act? You shot him down at the dance. You made it really clear you aren't going to do anything to help him meet your dad or get an audition or anything. What if he was so mad, he convinced the other guys to flake on the cheerleading completely—even at the game? None of them wanted to do it anyway, right?"

"A couple did—Ben and David," Joanna answered. "And Dr. Steve ordered the rest of them to do it as a punishment, remember?"

"It's the last day of the reunion," Sarah reminded her. "What's Dr. Steve going to be able to do about them ducking out?"

"I'm sure he'd figure out something when camp starts up in the summer," Natalie said. She looked at Sarah. "You really think Peter would sabotage the Spirit Award just to get back at me?"

"I don't know," Sarah answered. "I just want you to be prepared if the guys don't show up at all. I'm afraid it could happen. I just don't trust Peter."

"He'd have to really hate me to do something like that," Natalie said.

Sarah shrugged. "To me, it seems like Peter only likes people who can help him. If you can't do anything for him, he's done with you. He hasn't said a word to me this whole weekend. He didn't even apologize." Sarah kicked at the snow. "It's like I'm not even worth talking to because I don't really have a famous dad."

Natalie had really wanted to do something great for Walla Walla. Would Peter have been able to convince the guys to desert her?

She shook her head. Those guys were her friends. She'd known them forever. Yeah, they'd totally goofed off at practice. But they'd still show. They had to. Natalie picked up her pace. The football field was just around the next bend in the trail. *The guys will already be there*, she told herself. *They will. They've got to be.*

She began to jog. She had to see. She rounded the corner.

Almost the whole Walla Walla powder-puff team was already there. The Talamini team was there, too, all dressed in blue jerseys with TALAMINI TORNADOES printed on the front. No glitter or sequins for them. The Talamini cheerleaders were out in force, and, unlike the girls, they'd brought the bling. Natalie was pretty sure a couple of them had on sparkling blue false eyelashes, and all of them wore high gloss blue nail polish. Bunches of fans filled the bleachers for both teams.

There wasn't one Walla Walla cheerleader in sight. *I've completely failed as a coach*, Natalie thought. *I couldn't even get my squad to show up.*

"The game hasn't started yet. They could still come," Joanna told Natalie when she and Sarah caught up to her.

"Nat, if they don't come, it's nothing about you, okay?" Sarah gave Natalie's shoulder a pat. "I've got to go warm up with the team."

"We'll be cheering for you," Joanna promised as Sarah veered off toward the section of the field where the Walla Walla team was gathered.

"Let's sit close to the front," Natalie suggested when they reached the bleachers. "I want our cheering to sound as loud as possible." In case there weren't going to be any actual cheerleaders.

Sloan joined them as soon as they sat down. "Look at the way the sun is hitting the snow kitty," she said.

Natalie looked over. The snow sculpture glittered. It looked gorgeous. But there was another sight she'd rather have seen. Where were the guys? If they were going to show, they'd be here by now. Wouldn't they?

"It doesn't look like our cheerleaders are coming," Sloan commented as if she'd read Natalie's mind. "But we have lots of reasons to have our happy faces on. The fact that we're having the game at all. The beautiful, beautiful weather. Our great team."

Natalie forced a smile. Sloan was right. But somehow it didn't make her feel much better.

"It's starting!" Sloan exclaimed.

Dr. Steve and Mr. Billingham, the leader of Camp Talamini, were walking toward the center of the field. They shook hands. Mr. Billingham pulled out a quarter. He turned it back and forth in front of Dr. Steve's face.

"What's he doing?" Sloan asked.

Joanna laughed. Every time she laughed, Natalie had to smile. At least she'd managed to help Joanna enjoy part of the reunion. "I think he's proving to Dr. Steve that he's not using a two-headed coin," Joanna explained.

Mr. Billingham tossed the coin. It flashed in the sunshine. He caught it, then pointed to Talamini. They chose to receive.

"Sadly, that's the right decision," Sloan said. "Sarah's nickname is 'The Hands.' She can catch anything. And she's fast. She's great at interceptions."

"She'll get her chance," Joanna answered.

Chelsea knelt down and held the ball in position. Molly, a Walla Walla girl a year ahead of Natalie and her friends, moved into position. Natalie held her breath as she made the kick.

"Go, Sweet Kitties!" Natalie yelled as Tornado number 5 angled toward the ball and Avery angled toward her.

"Sweet Lil' Kitties," Joanna corrected, laughing again. "You can't leave out the *lil'*."

Bam! Avery hit number 5 just as her fingers grasped the ball. Fumble!

And Priya was right there waiting for it. She snatched the ball before it hit the ground and powered it down the field.

Jenna blocked one of the Tornadoes gunning for Priya. Chelsea and Shawn tag-teamed another one and brought her to a full stop. Priya made it to the thirty-yard line before she got tackled.

"Way to go, Priya!" Joanna shouted, leaping to her feet along with the other Walla Walla-ers, who were clapping and hooting and screaming like crazy.

Joanna leaned close to Natalie. "Our side yelled really loud. We don't need cheerleaders. The camp's full of great cheerers."

"You're right," Natalie answered.

Then the Talamini cheerleaders got out in front of the Talamini bleachers.

"Hey, hey, get out of our way!" the cheerleading guys chanted. "'Cause today is the day, we put you away!"

"Everybody!" one of the Talamini guys yelled. And every person in the Talamini bleachers joined in.

"Hey, hey, get out of our way! 'Cause today is the day we put you away!"

Compared to them, the Walla Walla crowd had been whispering. It made a huge difference when everyone was shouting the same words, instead of everyone yelling their own thing, the way the Walla Walla-ers had been doing.

Dr. Steve walked over and sat down next to Natalie and Joanna. "Where's our squad? Still fussing over their hair?" He smiled, but he looked a little worried.

"I don't know," Natalie had to admit. "I just . . . don't know."

Dr. Steve raised his eyebrows. "Haven't you two been working with them? You volunteered."

"We tried, but we—"

"Natalie did everything she possibly could!" Joanna interrupted.

Except get them to show up, Natalie thought. *We don't even have a shot at the Spirit Award now.*

chapter

We can still win the Sport Award, though, Natalie told herself as the Talamini captain hiked the ball to Talamini Tornado number 7. She faked right. Brynn went with the fake. Number 7 veered left. Tornado number 4 had broken out of the pack. She was in position for a pass.

Sarah was on her. She raced toward number 4, the glitter kitty on the back of her shirt sparkling. Number 7 threw the ball in a long, perfectly aimed arc straight for her teammate. Sarah cut in front of number 4, spun, leaped—and intercepted the ball!

It's like her hands were magnets and the ball was metal. It just came to her. At least that's how it looked.

Natalie jumped to her feet again. "Way to go, Sars!" she shouted. *Sarah deserved a real cheerleading squad,* Natalie thought. *All the Lil' Kitties did.* She promised herself that no matter how bad she was feeling about the guys pulling a no-show, she was going to cheer her best.

By halftime, Natalie's voice was hoarse and her hands hurt from clapping so hard. As soon as the girls were off the field, "All the Single Ladies" blasted out, and the Tornado cheerleaders pranced out to the center yard line. They spread out and started doing a move-by-move replication of Beyonce's video. Well, they were attempting move-by-move. They weren't quite getting there. But they were enthusiastic and everyone in the Talamini bleachers was going wild. A bunch of people were singing along, and some were dancing.

Dr. Steve applauded politely when the Tornado cheerleaders finished, but Natalie could tell he was disappointed that Walla Walla wasn't represented. Natalie was more than disappointed. She felt sick. She'd messed up so badly. There had to have been a way to get the guys motivated, and she hadn't found it.

Joanna patted her shoulder. "Stop thinking whatever you're thinking. You tried so hard. The guys just stink."

"And now, for your halftime entertainment—the Sweet Lil' Kitties cheerleaders."

"What?" Natalie exclaimed. Things were just getting worse and worse. There were no Sweet Lil' Kitties cheerleaders. Who had made that announcement? Maybe Dr. Steve and Mr. Billingham had worked out a halftime schedule and no one had—

"Look!" Joanna cried.

Natalie couldn't believe what she was seeing.

Peter led the cheerleaders out to the center of the field. They got into their starting positions in silence.

Let this plan work, he thought.

The sound of Jack Black singing "What's New Pussycat?"—most of it in Korean—ended the quiet. Peter smiled as he heard cheers and laughter. He'd thought choosing the song from that episode of *The Simpsons* had been pretty funny. Seemed like other people did, too.

The other good thing about the song—it was slow. That wasn't usually what cheerleading squads went for, but slow let the squad really get their moves in synch. And Peter thought he, David, and Ben had choreographed something cool. They'd put in lots of cat moves—claw hands, and swishing the boa tails they'd attached to their cheerleading skirts, and even a little bit where they licked their hands and ran them over one of their cat ears. Everybody had seen cats wash like that, and the fans seemed to like it as part of the routine. Peter definitely heard some whoops during that part.

Now it was time for the big finish, even though it felt like they'd only been on the field for a few moments. That happened to Peter sometimes when he was performing. All his awareness of time passing disappeared.

Peter moved into position. He and Ben were going to be the second level of the pyramid—what was, or was supposed to be at least, the power finish of the routine. They'd only managed to do it once in practice without somebody breaking their pose or falling. And they'd had to recruit one of the older guys, Rob, because they needed four people for the base. He'd agreed to participate in the pyramid only.

Yep, Rob was in place. Peter hoped it looked okay to have Rob run onto the field at the last minute. Too late to do anything about it. He stepped into the stirrups Miles and Justin had made by linking their hands. And pop. They boosted him onto their shoulders.

At the same moment, Conner and Rob boosted Ben up. *Perfect timing*, Peter thought. He felt Miles and Justin tighten their grips on his ankles. Peter stood as straight and steady as he could. Miles and Connor each had a free hand on the inside of the pyramid. Now they had to grab David and pop him up into his position with one foot on Peter's inside shoulder and one on Ben's.

Peter felt David's foot land, felt it wobble. He grabbed David's ankle to steady him. He felt a tremor go through the whole pyramid. A familiar feeling. The feeling that usually came right before the stack of bodies collapsed.

But David's foot felt solid now. And Miles and Connor still had good grips on each of Peter's feet. *It's gonna hold*, he thought. *It is holding!*

Peter couldn't stop himself from risking a real look at Natalie—finally. A huge grin was stretched across her face, and she was clapping. She looked completely happy.

But was she happy because the Walla Walla team had ended the half two points ahead? Or was she happy because his squad—*her* squad—was giving their all out on the field. Just the way Peter had planned they would.

Natalie blinked rapidly, half afraid the cheerleaders—with their cute little cat ears and cat tails—were some stress-induced hallucination. But blinking didn't make the boys disappear as they ran off the field and took their places in front of the Walla Walla bleachers. She struggled to force her attention onto the game as the third quarter started up.

"Ready, okay!" David yelled, jerking Natalie's attention back to the guys as the squad launched into one of the cheers Natalie had distributed to them:

"Don't wait!

Don't hesitate!"

Their arm movements weren't exactly crisp or precise. They weren't even quite in synch. But the cheer looked awesome to Natalie. She began to yell along with the squad as they continued to chant:

"For the battle has just begun.

Intimidate and dominate,

For the Sweet Lil' Kitties are number one!"

Natalie whooped as Ben did a cartwheel. The crowd went crazy when they spotted his boxers. They had GO, KITTIES, GO written on the back of them with purple puffy paint.

"Go, Kitties, Go!" everyone in the Walla Walla bleachers began to shout. "Go, Kitties, Go!"

The cheerleaders urged them on with fist pumps. Then Miles and Connor boosted Peter into a lift. He managed to get both his feet into position—one foot on each of their shoulders. Then he held it—with just a little wobbling. "Go, Kitties, Go!" he yelled before he let himself fall back. Justin and David made a basket out of their arms and caught him on the way down.

They let Peter bump his butt on the ground, but the move still looked good. Actually, to Natalie, it looked fantabulous!

Peter tried to keep his complete focus on the game. He'd found a cheerleading manual—from the seventies—on one of the lodge's massive bookshelves. It had emphasized that good cheerleading began with reacting to the plays. To do that, you had to actually pay attention.

He was having a little trouble with that. His eyes kept wanting to slip over to Natalie. Peter wanted to know if his plan had worked. Had getting the cheerleading squad pulled together made her happy? Happy enough to stop hating him?

There wasn't time to figure it out. His sister had just made a killer catch. Who knew Avery had it in her? He should have. When his twin put her mind to something, she usually rocked.

He and the guys launched into a simple cheer, leading the crowd in spelling out Avery's name.

"Do you think the Talamini guys have us beat?" David asked when they finished the cheer.

Peter shrugged. "Probably," he admitted. "But we did what we could with the time we had left."

Sloan gripped her hands so tightly together she could feel her knuckles aching in protest. Last quarter. Score: 17–16. With the 17 being the Tornadoes. There wasn't much time on the clock. A little. Enough to flip that score to a Sweet Lil' Kitties victory, if everything went perfectly.

Perfect didn't happen that often, though. And the Tornadoes had control of the ball. Or they did—until Avery made an awesome tackle!

"We won! I mean we're going to win. But we've pretty much already won!" Sloan exclaimed.

"Wait. Why?" Joanna asked.

"Avery just tackled that Tornado in the Tornadoes' end zone. That means we get two points, which puts us in the lead—and we get control of the ball," Sloan explained.

"They can still get it back though, right?" Joanna looked a little confused.

Football rules were a little confusing. But Sloan had them down. She'd been playing scorekeeper during the practices. "The last quarter is almost over. We can run down the clock now—thanks to Avery making that beast of a tackle. All we have to do is set the ball down a couple times."

"Yeah!" Sloan yelled as Sarah hiked the ball to Molly, and Molly immediately dropped to the ground with it, using up some of the very little time left. When the game resumed, the Kitties repeated the move. The air horn went off. Time was up. The game was over.

Everybody in the Walla Walla bleachers went nuts—hugging one another, cheering, and Sloan even spotted Natalie crying a few happy tears.

For a moment, Sloan thought she'd started to happy-cry, too. Then she realized the wet spot on her face was from a snowflake. She looked up. It was snowing, and the flakes were coming faster and faster.

Didn't matter. The game was over. And Walla Walla had won!

Sloan stuck out her tongue and caught one of the beautiful flakes on her tongue. "Thank you," she whispered to the sky. "Thanks for giving us this incredible day."

chapter THIRTEEN

"Ooooh," Natalie said, along with half the people in the dining room. Some people had gone with the equally appropriate, "aaaah."

The head cook for Walla Walla and the head cook for Talamini were rolling a cart with a huge cake on it to the front of the room. It was shaped like a football stadium, with marzipan players, cheerleaders, and fans.

"It's like something straight out of *Cake Boss*," Avery told Chelsea. They were wearing identical sweaters. Black. Cashmere. Banded hem and cuffs. With a tree made out of brass studs on the back.

"It so does," Chelsea agreed. She and Avery smiled identical smiles.

"Wow. We should have a trophy for that cake," Mr. Billingham called out as the cake cart came to a stop next to him. Everybody—Talamini-ites and Walla Walla-ers—applauded.

"Unfortunately, we don't," Dr. Steve added. "But our compliments to the chefs. Or should I call them *artistes*?"

"We do have these two to give out, though." Mr. Billingham gestured to the two gleaming gold trophies on the table between him and Dr. Steve.

"Let's start with Sports," Dr. Steve suggested. *No matter what happens with the Spirit Award, Walla Walla gets to take home one trophy*, Natalie thought.

Dr. Steve reached for the Sports trophy. Mr. Billingham put his hand on top of it protectively. "I just have a few words to say first," Mr. Billingham announced. He picked up the trophy and held it up in front of his face. "Don't worry," he told the trophy. "You'll be home where you belong before you know it." He turned the trophy so it was facing the group gathered in front of him.

"Talamini, Talamini, Talamini, Talamini, Talamini," Mr. Billingham said, touching some of the small plaques on the trophy that had his camp's name engraved on them.

"Sarah, Jenna, why don't you two come up and accept the trophy for your team," Dr. Steve suggested.

Mr. Billingham gave a loud mock—or mostly mock—howl as they approached him. He cradled the trophy in his arms. Sarah showed him no mercy. With Jenna's help, she pried the trophy away from him, to cheers from all the Walla Walla campers.

Natalie's stomach tensed up. She wasn't sure which camp would win the Spirit Award. Her guys—she still thought of them as hers, even though she hadn't helped them with the routines they'd ended up performing— had done a great job. But the Talamini cheer boys had been super enthusiastic, too. And neither squad had presented a truly polished routine. How could they, with so few days to prep?

Days mostly unused by my guys, Natalie thought. They must have worked like demons to have pulled everything together—the costumes and the choreography, the music, and just their whole attitude. *And they skipped all the snow fun to do it*, she realized. It just clicked into her head. That's why they hadn't been outside that morning—they'd been rehearsing.

"Okay, onto the Spirit Award." Dr. Steve rubbed his hands together. "Even Mr. Billingham and I don't know who won. We invited a few locals—without ties to either of our camps—to judge."

Mr. Billingham waved an envelope over his head. "The name of the winning camp is right in here."

"Open it!" one of the Talamini cheerleaders yelled.

"Yes, please open it!" Natalie called out. If she had to wait much longer, she'd explode. Or implode. Whichever it was, it wouldn't be fun, or pretty.

"This? You want me to open this?" Mr. Billingham teased, making a tiny rip in the envelope flap.

The crowd went psycho. People started shouting all over the dining room. "Yes!" "Do it" "Come on, Mr. Billingham!"

Mr. Billingham grinned and passed the envelope to Dr. Steve. "Why don't you do the honors?"

Dr. Steve finished opening the envelope with one long rip. He pulled out a sheet of paper and unfolded it. Then he held it up for everyone to see. The winner was written on the piece of paper in bright red letters: CAMP WALLA WALLA!

Natalie didn't plan to stand up, but, somehow, she was on her feet, cheering and cheering.

Mr. Billingham made a grab for the trophy, but this time Dr. Steve was too fast for him. He snatched it up. "Somebody come up here and get this thing," Dr. Steve exclaimed. "I don't know how long I can keep Mr. Billingham off it!"

"You do it, Natalie!" David yelled.

"Natalie, Natalie, Natalie!" the other guys started to chant.

"Get up there, Nat," Joanna told her.

Natalie, feeling a little dazed, hurried to the front of the room and took the Spirit trophy from Dr. Steve. "I have to say, even though I was supposed to be coaching the guys, they really did this on their own," Natalie said. "I'm so proud of them! And I'm so proud Camp Walla Walla will be keeping this trophy!"

"For the year," Mr. Billingham put in.

Natalie winked at him. "We'll see about that!"

"Okay, let's get this cake cut," Dr. Steve said.

Natalie started back to her table. Then she paused. She had to know how the squad . . . became a squad. And not just any squad, but a squad good enough to win the Spirit trophy.

She headed for the boys' table. All the boys were there except Peter, who was busy congratulating his sister on her awesome game. David jumped up and rushed over to Natalie. He swung her around in a hug.

"You guys were awesome," Natalie told him. "Congratulations!" She leaned over David's shoulder, grinning at the rest of the squad. "Congratulations, you guys!"

"You were surprised, I bet," David said.

"Yeah. Honestly—I still don't know how you pulled it together," Natalie admitted. She looked over at Miles. "I wasn't sure you'd be able to get in front of a crowd without puking."

"I almost didn't," Mile admitted. "But the deep breathing techniques Peter taught me saved my butt."

"Peter did pretty much everything. He whipped us into shape," David told her.

"Peter? Really?" Natalie asked. "If I had to guess, I'd have said you or Ben. You're the only two who even wanted to cheer."

"It wasn't about wanting to cheer," David said. "It was about you. Peter did it for you."

"Impossible," Natalie told him. "That last practice—he was completely mocking me. He made everything ten times worse."

David raised his eyebrows. "That's what you think?" He shook his head. "Peter wasn't mocking you. I guess, yeah, he did say a lot of the same things you'd said at the other practice. But he was serious. He was trying to give us a kick in the butt, get us working."

Natalie didn't know what to say to that. She just stared at David for a few moments, then glanced over at Peter. He was already looking at her. His expression was . . . hopeful.

"He likes you, Nat. That's why he did it," David said. "He even had to give away all the DVDs he brought with him as bribes. Not that we all needed to be bribed."

"Some of us did, though. And we enjoyed it," Justin volunteered. "I now have my very own copy of

Evil Dead 2, which I will have to keep hidden from my parents along with the rest of my contraband."

"That was . . . it really didn't . . . the cake is getting passed around," she told David. "I have to get back to my table." She hurried back to her chair and sat down.

Joanna held out her hand for a high five. "Yay, Natalie! We got the Spirit Award!"

"David said Peter got the guys organized. He even gave some of the guys DVDs to get them to do it," Natalie said.

"Peter gave away DVDs?" Avery asked. "That's true devotion. He loves his movie collection."

"I don't get it," Natalie said. She rubbed her forehead with her fingertips. "It's making my brain hurt." Could Peter really *like* her, the way David said?

An answer whispered through her mind, turning her whole body cold. *Or is this just another attempt by Peter to get to my dad and turn the whole thing into an acting job opportunity?*

"Nat, what if it's all for your dad?" Sarah asked softly, echoing Natalie's own dark thoughts.

"It's not," Avery said. "I know you don't have any reason to believe that, but it's true. He likes you, Natalie."

Sarah let out a long sigh, but she didn't comment. *Sarah really believed Peter liked her*, Natalie thought. *She was totally convinced.* More convinced than Natalie was that Peter truly liked her.

Natalie nibbled on her bottom lip. Peter was still really into being an actor. That hadn't changed. And her dad could help him out—if Natalie asked him to. That was a huge motivation for him to have done what he did.

But what he did—it was pretty amazing. Natalie made a decision. She had to at least talk to Peter.

Natalie stood up.

"Don't, Nat," Sarah said.

But she had to.

▲ ▲ ▲

Peter knew Natalie was heading toward him. Some part of his brain was always monitoring where she was and what she was doing.

And she was stopping. Now she was standing still about halfway between her table and his.

Peter couldn't take it. He shoved back his chair, got up, and strode over to her before he could change his mind. He had to know what she was thinking— good or bad. "Hi," he said. Not anywhere near the perfect line for this scene, but it's all he could come up with. It sucked that real life couldn't be scripted.

If it could, Natalie would completely understand why he'd worked so hard with the squad. If it could, he wouldn't need to apologize because she'd already know how bad he felt about the way he treated Sarah, and the way he'd tried to use Natalie's dad.

"I really messed up last year," he told Natalie. He really didn't want to talk about the badness. He wished they could all just forget about it. But Peter had finally figured out that wasn't going to happen. "I was really selfish. I used Sarah. And I would have used you if I'd known you were really Tad Maxwell's daughter."

Peter sucked in a quick breath and went on. He didn't want to give Natalie time to answer, not until he'd said everything. "I know I hurt Sarah. And I know I hurt you. And it was all so maybe I could score an acting job. I'm sorry, Natalie. I'm really, really sorry. I'm going to apologize to Sarah, too."

Now he wanted Natalie to say something. Anything. Not knowing what she was thinking was killing him.

"So you pulled the squad together as a way of making it up to us?" Natalie finally asked, her blue eyes somber.

"Yeah. Yeah, but that wasn't the only reason," Peter answered. He was going to be all about the truth, the whole truth, and nothing but the truth.

"David said it was because you . . . David said it was because you like me," Natalie said, before Peter had had a chance to figure out how to tell her exactly the same thing. That he liked her. A lot.

"It's true," he answered. He cleared his throat. It had gone a little dry.

"We barely know each other." Natalie crossed her arms. "I feel like the only thing you know about me is who my father is."

"Not true," Peter protested.

"Really? Tell me something else you know about me," Natalie challenged.

Peter's mind went totally blank. All he could do was stare.

"Yeah, I can tell it's totally not true," Natalie snapped. "Don't ever talk to me again." She started to turn away from him, but Peter caught her by the elbow.

"I like that," he blurted out.

Natalie frowned. "What?"

"I like how you say what you think," Peter explained. "I like how you don't let anyone get away with anything. Right now it's kind of annoying because I'm not trying to get away with anything, no matter what you think. But even now I kind of like it."

Natalie didn't say anything. But she didn't pull away.

"I know you're kind of cute when you're mad," he added in a rush. Why did everything that came out of his mouth sound so fake? When he was acting, he could make anything sound real. But now when he was trying to tell the truth, he was afraid it sounded like he was trying to con her.

He was relieved to see Natalie's lips twitch with a suppressed smile. It gave him the courage to go on. "I know you're a good dancer. I know you're a loyal friend. And I know when you do something, you give it your all."

"Kind of seems like you do, too. I know it couldn't have been easy getting that squad together," Natalie told him, a small smile spreading across her face.

"Yeah, I usually go all out when I want something. I have a new rule, though. Getting what I want can't involve hurting anyone else," Peter added.

"Good rule—if you're really going to follow it," Natalie said. "Look, I want to believe you. I'm even heading toward believing you. But I need some time."

Peter nodded. Some of the tension in his body relaxed. "So, maybe I could call you sometimes, before camp starts up in the summer. Or e-mail you."

Natalie gave a full-on smile. "I like that plan."

So did Peter. He really, really liked that plan because he really, really liked Natalie.

EPILOGUE

Posted by: Avery
Subject: My Sweater

Chelsea, I think you accidentally went home with my sweater. You know the one—black, cashmere, tree made out of brass studs on the back.

Please return. I'd let you keep it, but I don't think it's really your style.

Kisses,

Avery

Posted by: Joanna
Subject: Sorries!!

Sorry if I was kind of cold during part of the reunion. (Pun totally intended.) I was just worried about my mom being all alone while she was recovering from her surgery. I have to remember that she has a ton of friends who are there for her the same way you are all there for me. Somebody was over at the house every day.

And this weekend all her friends are taking her,

and me, out to dinner at our favorite place—Big Poppa's. They have the most amazing seafood. But that's not the best part. The best part is that my mom asked my dad if he wanted to come—since they are also friends and all (or at least attempting to be)—and he said yes.

Sorry again! Can't wait for summer—warm, warm, wonderful summer.

Joanna

Posted by: Chelsea
Subject: My Sweater

Well, Miss Avery, I did make it home with a sweater like the one you described. But it can't belong to you. It fits me too perfectly and looks too fab on me to belong to anyone else. Check your stuff. I think you might have accidentally gone home with my sweater.

Chels

Posted by: Brynn
Subject: Joanna

We're all cool! (Pun intended, even though it wasn't a very good one.)

Brynn

Posted by: Jenna
Subject: Meow-roar

Just wanted to let you all know that Sarah and I have been e-mailing each other ideas for plays for next year's powder-puff game. (Joanna, you are a key part of several of them, so bring your long underwear. We love you—even though you should have just told us what was the matter right away!) We aren't going to let Talamini get that trophy back until we've broken the five-year record. That means we'll be at camp together until we're in college. Yay!

Jenna

Posted by: Avery
Subject: My twin

Just an update on my not-so-better half. Peter's still spending almost all his time in his man cave. But he isn't watching movies all the time, the way he used to. Nope. He's on his computer, making little videos. Videos of Luuurve for a certain someone. He's also writing e-mails and making phone calls to the girl.

BTW, I am ignoring all future sweater posts. We all know in our hearts what is true. (And that is that the sweater in question looks better on me, so I should have both of them. Chelsea, you have my address.)

Avery

Posted by: Natalie
Subject: that girl

that girl avery was talking about has been enjoying the phone calls, e-mails, and videos. (although she'd call them videos of hope. or videos of like.)

that girl avery was talking about wants to give

a shout out to another girl you might know. if you need someone to get your back, she's awesome at it. she's also awesome at knowing that people can change. and forgiving those people.

later, okay? i'm expecting a phone call!

nat

Posted by: Sarah
Subject: Awesomeness

Just so we're clear, I am the girl Natalie was talking about. I am awesome in all ways. And I'm available for any back-getting or other acts of friendship any of you need!

Sarah

Posted by: Sloan
Subject: Intentions

Hey, guys, I went to another lecture with my parents and my aunt Willow. (Yes, it was a lecture of the woo-woo variety.) Anyway, turns out sending your intentions out to the universe can affect more than the weather. It can affect anything and everything!

So, tomorrow at 4:00 (Walla Walla time), I want us all to intend—just wish hard, the way we did about having the perfect day for the powder-puff game—that this summer at Walla Walla will be our best ever!!!

Peace, Love, and Light (and Sweet Lil' Kitties),

Sloan